The False Fae

After the Old World, Volume 1

Ausar Imani

Published by Ausar Imani, 2022.

THE FALSE FAE

First edition. December 12, 2022.

Copyright © 2022 Ausar Imani.

ISBN: 979-8987156513

Written by Ausar Imani.

Table of Contents

Dedication

To those who listened to me even when I thought my voice had nothing to offer. I hope to honor the value and faith you have placed in me. I cherish you all dearly; my family, professors, mentors, brothers, and my love.

Preface

If you had asked me ten years ago if this book would have ever been written, I would have called you a fool. Not because I think it isn't very reasonable to tell stories when it feels like everything has already been said a thousand times, but because I never thought storytelling mattered. Some timeless works have expressed the foundation of our very being and entertained us, while others have created voids between others and caused us to damn the *other*. We are beings cursed and blessed by our self-awareness, and stories resonate with us through the journey of learning to be ourselves. From simple poems to lyrical masterpieces and parables to film, storytelling is a creative outlet that helps us express parts of ourselves we see and have yet to find. This book is my attempt to find myself and communicate details I don't know are my own or the influence of the world I've come to love.

The False Fae is the first part in the *After the Old World* Series and is a homage to everything found significant about myths and legends that have fueled human culture and history with a touch of Science-Fiction. My goal is to create a robust universe that is familiar and unfamiliar to those with experience with Fantasy themes. Having met so many people with different perspectives on life, I hope to continue to push the boundaries of storytelling and challenge readers to see how big the world is. Ethics and morality have often fascinated me, and I want to see how it holds up in a world that acts as an amalgamation of diversity and philosophical thought. Also, I want to write about awesome weirdos and people doing extraordinary things because my imagination rivals a spider hooked on caffeine.

The False Fae Vol. I: Revelations and Beyond

By Ausar Imani

Cover Art By

Alexaelartworks

THE FORGOTTEN MEMORIA

The feeling of something cold and sharp piercing my abdomen made me jump up and clench my gut. I couldn't utter a single word or see anything; there was only darkness. My shallow breath only made the pain that covered my body ache more. A part of me almost chuckled at how painful being stabbed is. Even though it wasn't my first time, I had an unconscious reaction to flinch at the pain. I could hear the words, "How many more times?" echo in my head. I knew it wasn't about my recent traumatic experience, but I could not remember why else I thought about those words. I knew everything after "this" would be a friggin drag.

As I lay on my side, trying to catch my breath, my vision returned, and the pain slowly faded. I rose to my knees and the blurred colorless outlines of the world formed as if someone was sketching the globe before my eyes. Gradually, the blackened rocks took shade, and I realized I was in a dark cavern. The sprawled seams across the walls and floor revealed golden flames that looked too familiar. Although I could feel the warmth from its rough surface as it emitted the gold hue, it made my body shiver. I had seen that gold light so many times, but what should have given me a sense of wonder left a typical yet bitter taste in my mouth.

As I focused on the crusty veins of the walls, I noticed how much they resembled the inside of a volcanic area. The only difference was light surging through the crust instead of lava. The light was like the fires that covered my hands, but I noticed how the flames on me flickered between black, white, and gold. As usual, there was no pain when I had these flames. They had always kept me safe when I needed them, but originally it was more than a hassle to use them. Now, turning them on and off was like breathing.

As they faded, my mind showed blurred images, fragmented stills of what I assumed were my memories. Even as they flashed by, I felt nothing, yet I grasped my chest, expecting to feel something. I still could recall who I was; however, there was a gap in my memory of how I had come here. Although I knew there was nothing I could do about the situation, that didn't stop me from wanting to complain about it. Then again, if I did, no one would hear me.

Instead of thinking about my circumstances, I pressed forward, placing my hands on a nearby wall. The grittiness of the wall's sharp edges scraped against my hand, and instantly they conflagrated in the golden hue again. And again, that bitterness swelled in my chest. No memories arose as I continued to think about why I was here. Only the urge to hit something and furiously rage occupied my mind. As I progressed, the area's color suddenly changed from soft gold to deep violet. The shift was so jarring it forced my eyes shut. When they opened again, I saw a wide-open space with an enormous tree. So huge looking at it left a crick in my neck from where I stood. Although my mind and heart were a mess, I understood how "awe" felt.

As my eyes continued upwards, I saw a nebula of stars, odd shapes, and large orbital bodies. "Beautiful" was the only word that crossed my mind. My memories showed stars were standard in the night sky, but something about them gave me a sense of comfort. I was seeing everything against the midnight backdrop left me awe-stricken—everything except a ring in the center. A pitch-black void lay in the middle of a white circle that contrasted the darkness. Somehow it looked as if everything was flowing and falling into its epicenter.

My eyes dropped back to the tree, avoiding the idea of staring too long into the abyss. I didn't know anything about that abyss, but something told me I wanted nothing to do with it. When my eyes landed on my hands, they were shaking. Instead of focusing on those feelings, my mind centered on the large tree surrounded by smaller trees in the distant grove. I could feel my eyes strain as they focused on the distant tree. Suddenly my body pressed forward without my will.

I couldn't put my finger on what drew me in with every step, but for some reason, I knew this wasn't my first time. Something eerily familiar about that tree made my body shiver wild enough to lose footing, but I continued to ignore it. Getting closer to the smaller trees, I could see a large gem that glowed in the center of each one. I wanted to touch them, but my hands shook violently. The trees seemed just as otherworldly and made of the same material as the wall. Some of the trees even bore what appeared to resemble a crystal-like fruit.

As I gazed at the gems in their center, my hands touched one of them. It was as if someone were cutting out my memories and stitching in new ones at a blinding speed. My memories were no longer my own, sights of buildings that stretched into the sky, battlefields of bodies laid across the ground, tears from feelings I couldn't comprehend; at that moment, I felt as if I had experienced the lives of thousands of beings. Continuous cycles of death and rebirth had flown by in a second.

Jolting back, I fell and began convulsing. The aching in my head grew a thousand-fold, feeling like it would shatter into dust. It took a few seconds to regain my footing, and my body automatically continued through the grove. After that moment, I knew touching the fruit was a terrible idea. Déjà vu told me I hadn't learned my lesson and was prey to a typical mistake. Gold flames flooded my body, calming me down before they disappeared again. The endless flow of those memories rushing through my mind made me want to smash my head in, but I knew I had to keep going.

I felt myself breaking with every step, pain spiked, and my mind shattered like glass crashing into the floor. Beings with pointed ears, winged creatures with scales, overgrown insects, and forms my mind couldn't comprehend suddenly popped into my head. Now, I could no longer remember what I had done. Instead, my mind drifted to visions of all those other entities and their lives. Moments that I knew nothing of ran through my mind in unfamiliar languages. Even their emotions washed over me. I could no longer remember the first time I felt sadness, happiness, or anger—instead, the memories and feelings of thousands replaced my own.

My fingers pierced my head as I screamed, but I could not hear a sound. Who was I? Why am I here? Anything involving my home was disappearing. I did not even know what my life resembled or who was a part of it. Constantly I tried to push away unfamiliar sights of someone else's life, but they returned, trying to drown out who I thought was me. Everything began to blur in my head, and I could no longer feel my feet beneath me as they took every step. Somehow it felt as if I was watching myself move on my own. Even so, the desire to reach that central tree compelled me.

As I walked forward, many trees were zipping by, and they all looked the same. As I turned behind me, a sea of trees rose, leaving no sight of how I had entered. It felt as if hours had passed, yet I made zero progress. I stumbled into a sprint, but only more trees and random memories flowed in and out of my focus. With more time passing by, those memories slowly began isolating. My mind centered, and my legs started to move faster and faster. Now swifter than the wind, my eyes focused, and my body became mine again. I ran left and then right several times, passing more trees repeatedly. Even though this felt endless, somehow, my body knew where it was going.

I finally arrived at the grove's center when all hope seemed lost. The tree was far more massive from the front than I could have ever imagined. Its summit was high enough to block out the sky, and the edge of its trunk was impossible to see from up close. By some remarkable chance, the moment I touched the tree, it forced all those memories away. I could finally feel my chest rising and falling with every breath. The peace of mind was so beautiful that I kissed the friggin tree.

I continued walking around the giant tree, staring into the upper canopy and whistling. The large branches above shimmered with crystal-like fruit, like the smaller trees I had seen before. They were like the stars in the sky, and their beauty reminded me of someone. Even though I couldn't see who they were, their silhouette made my heart flutter. Shortly after, that throbbing became spiteful, but a smile stretched across my face and faded just as quickly.

After a bit, I saw a person lying asleep on one of its lower branches if you could call her that. Most of the memories referred to individuals that resembled her structure as "People" or "Aos-Si." Still, it was hard to believe she was human, with skin as dark as the night sky and snow-white hair that outlined her slumbering body. The sight of her unfazed by the surrounding world made a chuckle escape my mouth. The scene before resembled watching a cat napping under the sun.

Suddenly I saw the same image replay in my mind, but instead of this decayed volcano scenery, it was a blue-lit forest under a starry night sky. Instead of white hair and black skin, I saw scarlet hair and pale ivory skin. The images switched back and forth, making me clench my head and lean on the tree. My heart ached, I wanted to rip the world apart, and at the same time, I wanted to hold "her" one last time. I couldn't recall who she was, but I knew she made me feel many things, especially hate and love.

Before I could completely process my feelings, the rattling sound of metal caught my attention. Without warning, a chain launches from the ground in a flash, barely grazing me and causing blood to spurt from my cheek. However, it wasn't blood but a gold-like substance when I took a second look. The pain from the cut was intense, but I brushed it off. Unfazed, I leaped backward and saw her eyes glaring at me.

Like the area's light, her eyes were a bedazzling violet, shimmering like the crystal from the tree. Focusing too hard on her, I realized I had put too much force into my jump. When I landed, my feet stumbled, and I didn't even notice something supporting me from behind. I turned around, and our eyes met with her hand at the center of my back. She was in two places at once, lying in the tree and breaking my fall.

Looking at her eyes again, I felt an intense burning sensation in my chest like before. If I could put it into words, she was captivating. Even though she stared at me as if I were prey to a beast, I was mesmerized. My blood was running cold, yet I couldn't prevent my eyes from focusing on her lips. Swiftly my sight went back to her eyes, and I hopped away. She practically stared into my soul, making me uncertain how to respond.

"I don't think I've seen another living creature here in quite some time," she spoke.

My mouth opened and closed without words leaving my lips. I couldn't understand what made me hesitate to utter a single word. With those eyes still locked onto me, I knew I had to say something; I didn't know what to say. After taking a deep breath and letting anything slip from my mouth, I spoke with as much confidence as possible.

"Who or what are you?"

"Who?" She pauses. "Ah... It has been quite some time since I spoke my name. What is yours?"

"I am—"

That phrase repeated a dozen times before realizing I no longer knew my name. I believed I had traveled across a land called Abhainn-Reatha, but even that became foggy. What I had done there and who I met started to fade from my mind. All I could remember was my favorite color was gray, spicy food made my world go round, and redheads scared me senseless.

I couldn't imagine why I would wander to such a place for my life; I only hope it's worth it. It felt like I lived vicariously by someone else who told me of myself. Dwelling on that made my shoulder droop with a heavy sigh. Before I realized I had spaced out, that woman disappeared. As I turned, looking around for her, I saw she was only sitting in the tree. Her face was utterly relaxed, yet I still felt intimidated.

When I touched my chest and felt my heart pumping harder, I realized the other feeling I felt was fear. Regardless of that fear, something unknown drew me to that mysterious woman. I looked up the tree and visualized the path I would take to reach her. It felt like sweat dripped down my face, but nothing was there when I used my hand to wipe it. Suddenly my hand looked utterly different. My skin was gone, and it glowed like gold flames. Slowly my entire body was beginning to burn like my fire. A sharp pain shot through my head and enveloped my body, leaving my mind hazier.

"Your memories are already beginning to fade. Soon only your Memoria will be left."

My gaze darted at her, "Fan-friggin-tastic. Why is this a thing?"

Her hands pointed behind me, and other entities were wandering the area like magic. A few were made of pure black fire, while others were white or gold. It seemed my vision was playing tricks on me. I couldn't tell if they had been there the whole time or if it was some spell she was doing. The flame-like beings roamed, bumping around into every tree they passed, howling as they flailed on the ground. As the two of them collided with each other, they fought. A black one engulfed a white one and screeched in an unfamiliar language. Its cries made my body shiver, paralyzing my movements. I could see its belly digesting the white fires.

"This place feeds on your memories; if you're a spirit, it takes them even faster."

She was far away, but her voice was as straightforward as she was next to me. I didn't know whether she meant this strange place or if those creatures fed on my memories, but I didn't plan on staying here long enough to find out. I knew I was getting out even if I didn't know how I got here. Quickly I got into a crouching position, preparing to leap toward the tree where she lay. I pranced towards her as my gold flames illuminated my feet more. With their glow, I felt a vibration resonating from the ground.

The flames heightened my body's senses, allowing me to perceive the chains rumbling through the crust. Although I didn't understand why I could feel those chains, I didn't friggin care. The way I hopped every other second, outmaneuvering them as they rose from the ground, made me feel badass. It was like my body was moving on its own. I knew I wanted to move forward, but everything else happening felt like someone else was responding to the assault. Even so, I was still impressed. When I got to the tree's trunk, they also sprouted from it. It was unexpected, but I parried the chains as they flew out of the tree.

"Are you trying to kill me, woman!?"

I hopped and launched myself towards a lower branch, consistently knocking three more aside. I had noticed a pattern of six in each volley. As I turned in midair, I saw three rising from the ground. I knocked away two and caught the last one as a ride upward. I was surprised that my hands could grasp them, yet in my mind, I knew there wasn't anything these flames couldn't touch or manipulate. As cheesy as that sounded, I thought it was fantastic. Regardless, these flames and their abilities were now a mystery to me.

Before another volley of the chains appeared, I had landed on the same branch the mysterious woman sat on. Looking back down, I saw thousands of those fires wandering below, and I had no idea what they were and what was going on. I took a deep to calm myself, and as I walked towards her, she spoke to me with that piercing glare.

"So, you're a Sibuna Adnero wielder? You must know how how you've arrived here?"

I was still in awe of not dying, but my train of thought was interrupted by the word "Adnero." My brain scrambled to find that word's meaning and looked for words to assuage a being that could disappear faster than my perception. My sight dropped to the flames my body emitted, and I knew its name was Adnero Sibuna. There were the flames of manipulation, a type of magic long forgotten in the land of Abhainn-Reatha. It was so old, magic wasn't the word used to describe it; "Ars" was.

"I'm not sure, realm goddess. I was hoping you could tell me."

"Goddess? That is a bold assumption to state. Even with that latent snark in your voice."

I couldn't tell there was a sense of snark in my tone, but she could. Oddly enough, she didn't kill me over it, so it must not offend her.

"Celestials have long passed from this dominion; I am simply Transcendent. Only you and your master would know that" she continued.

Suddenly my mind recalled my master's old books. They said the Transcendents had a physical form in the metaphysical realm. They were beings who left the living world and found a way into the world beyond ours. From what I remembered, they could reach into the physical world and speak to those inside it if their presence were strong enough. A Transcendent had knowledge beyond space and time that superseded the greatest of sages. It's no wonder she knew about my gold flames, Adnero Sibuna. I gripped my head again and spoke aloud.

"Wait, my master? Adnero?"

Those other memories still overrode the sight of my master's face, but her outline reappeared. She wore a dress that made her look nun-like, contrasting her personality. Its royal blue color with white and gold trim contrasted her long flowing hair. Instantly the thought faded, and words kept flashing into my mind like a jumbled mess. Ideas, people, things, and places in my head spread across my mind like a table, yet almost nothing connected them.

The confusion forced my body to its knees as trying to stay aware was becoming too complicated. I shook my head, looking back at her as she stared at the crystallized fruit. Abruptly another blurry figure appeared. It was an image of an unfamiliar person with a sword and shield blocked by light. They pointed their sword at me, and even though their face was also blank, I felt the rage in their voiceless words.

"Sorry, I don't remember," I apologized.

Her hand beckoned me to come.

"Sit and tell me, what do you see?"

I was hesitant to walk toward her, but I didn't sense the chains in the branches of the trees. I knew I couldn't afford to be careless, so I proceeded with caution. After taking a step forward, my body suddenly sat in front of the fruit between us. Her abilities dumbfounded me, and I simply accepted I was already sitting down.

As I sat looking into the fruit, I saw a familiar face. It was the Fae Queen destined to be seated on Tir-noNog's throne. She sat with her curled raven black hair adorned with a silver crown next to a young child with thick wooly hair who was a near-splitting replica. The silver circlet had gems that matched the color of her violet eyes. The memory of her saving the land of Abhainn-Reatha flashed into my mind. Her name was Ninlil Anemone, the successor Queen of Tir-noNog. She was also the pain in my ass who ended my life.

...A day in the Oryza Prairie

The sounds of metal swiftly clashing echoed through the treetops of a dense forest. Small gales erupted from every collision, causing leaves to instantly flash into the air and shred apart. The evening sunshine peered through the forest's edge and caught the sparring warriors' eyes. After one sheathed his sword, the two stopped to notice the sun's orange hue slowly filling the sky. The second one followed suit and put her knives away, as the sight of a True Dragon flying over her head made her heart flutter.

"Sorry, Sprout." The older warrior turns to her, holding on to a knife strapped to his side, "I can't help but enjoy the autumnal season and sunsets in Oryza, especially now."

"I know Spriggan," the young Fae woman nodded.

The glowing sigils on her arms faded as they gazed into the horizon. Its lush foliage mimicked an endless sea of reds, yellows, and oranges to signal the season's change. Spriggan continued to stare into the distance, saying nothing. Around this time of year, Spriggan would become more sentimental than usual. She was aware of it, particularly when he gazed into the Oryza Prairie past their home. She could see there was something on his mind.

Even in the middle of random conversations, she would notice his usually boisterous demeanor slowly fade into a faint melancholy. The cold air broke her train of thought and made her shiver. A smile stretched from ear to ear as she saw the holes in the green dress. The dress was far better than she expected, but Spriggan shook his head.

"Titania will kill you when she sees what you've done to that dress, Anemone," he smirked.

"That's IF she finds out WE ruined it," Anemone added.

"You're blaming my combat training on your ability to get your nice clothes cut up." His brow raised.

"I can't help to wear such a color." Her chest puffed. "As a TirNog Fae, it shows my pride."

"It's far past the season for such color, Sprout. Even history says so."

"Did I forget to mention it's my *favorite* color?

Although the dress was a hand-me-down from her mother, Titania, Spriggan was right to worry for Anemone's sake. Titania had already warned her about ruining any more of her clothes. This dress had belonged to her great-grandmother Medb, and it was one that Titania had cherished dearly. Anemone, who had a distaste for their tradition of clothing colors matching the season, had run through nearly all her green clothing. Everyone wore green to represent the lush Spring season and Tir-noNog's prosperity. Knowing that the kingdom's history marked Autumn as a time of large-scale conflict, to her, green was a far better color to wear.

They were in far more peaceful times, so she felt it was no longer necessary to match colors to seasons. To her, wearing green, in contrast to the season, marked the "true" triumph of peace. After looking down again, she realized how tattered most of the green dress was. She would have been far colder if it weren't for her black leggings. Soon her shoulders slumped as the sight of the dress made her guilt swell. What was once her mother's lovely hand-me-down dress was now a tattered mini dress. She looked back at Spriggan with displeasure, and he could only scoff.

As they walked through the canopy, she thought of an excuse to lessen Titania's wrath, but then she wondered if she would care. The wind blew again; the beauty of the Autumn leaves blowing past the rolling hills caught her eyes and distracted her thoughts from their sparring.

Anemone loved Spriggan dearly, but she couldn't help but think of her. Staring into the distance, she dwelled on Titania traveling through the Oryza Prairie. She had been gone for some time, and Anemone was far more interested in what Titania was doing than how she felt about the dress. She wished it was Titania training her, but she was always away.

Spriggan had raised Anemone for as long as she could remember. Besides Hibernica and other tutors or vassals, he was her primary caretaker. He was like the grandfather she had never met. From her studies to her skills in combat, Spriggan was there every step of the way. Anemone knew she might have never held a weapon if it were not for him. Unlike Spriggan, Titania only wanted her to focus on her studies, and today he was revisiting one she hated Flux Diversity.

"You may see this as pointless, but this *Furin* will help you perceive the *Flux* of threats. Especially in these woods."

"Come on, Spriggan, the Seelie Woods isn't that scary. Besides, I'm good at sensing threats. It's fighting that's the issue."

"I'm not teaching you anything your *Flux* can't handle, Sprout. There's no point if you can't cast a Furin with your Od."

"Ugh... *Od Conversion* sucks, and it's so tiring! I wished those *feather heads* from Airemul taught me a thing or two."

"Unless you have Dragon's yolk, there's a fat chance a Tengu Avian will teach ya anything!" He smiled. "You'll just have to focus and clear your head instead."

Spriggan's usual snarking words frustrated her, but she was glad. Continuing to dwell on Titania was the last thing she wanted to do. With their sparring session concluded, she went into the lower branches of the Greater Elms to take a break. They had already checked the *Furin Bells* Ars in the surrounding area. It was a magical spell Spriggan placed around the outer perimeter of Tir-noNog in the Seelie Woods.

When the presence of something's *Flux* passes within a few meters of the *Furin Bells*, it sends a signal that only the user can hear. The vibrations matched the resonance of the caster *Flux* and signaled unfamiliar individuals approaching. It was an old-world *Sylph-Ars* he had learned from a Tengu Avian in the Dragovian kingdom of Airemul. It was a land way beyond the forest of Tir-noNog and far to the North. She always dreamed of visiting it, even if it was teeming with deadly flying creatures.

Spriggan climbed down as well and began meditating not too far from her. She knew there was no reason for them to rush back to Tir-noNog, so it was perfect timing to clear her mind. With no damage done to any of the sigils carved into the trees for the *Furin Bells*, she had time to sketch for a bit. Anemone grabbed a falling leaf and drew its veins. Soon she began drawing the scene of the falling star-shaped Scarlet Quercus leaves, focused on the colorful scenery. After that, she continued to watch the leaves fall. It was a simple pleasure to her but seeing the bright colors across the floor was beautiful. Her habit was often to space out and draw random things during academy lectures, especially plants.

Her eyes caught an acorn beginning to fall from a tree branch above. Once it dropped into her line of sight, her focus landed on her right forearm. A sigil reappeared and shined through her arm's sleeves. As she raised it, her muscles became thicker and far more hardened. When the acorn aligned with her arm, she timed her flick and sent it flying through the forest like an arrow.

"You've improved a lot, Sprout. It's nice to see your *Synergist-Ars* at work."

"Yeah, but boosting my speed and striking power isn't enough."

"Are you still conflicted over your lack of casting *Sylph-Ars*?"

Anemone sighed, "What kind of Fae has a *Flux* with no compatibility with *Sylph* Od?".

Spriggan retorted, "Sometimes that's just how Sprout. *Flux* works in mysterious ways. Besides, we—"

"We," she interrupted, "Have to work with what we have to make up for what we lack. The tree with the strongest roots bears the sweetest fruit."

"Yet I am forced to repeat my words."

"I can't help that I'm the daughter of the world's mightiest *Sylph* wielder," her voice groaned. "The Celestials have '*some*' sense of humor."

"Reaching Titania's level of skill takes years. She lacked your skill with Exalt or Analeptic-Ars even at your age."

She waved her quill around. "Support with *Synergist-Ars* is cool, but I wanna shoot tornadoes out of my hands, flood my foes, or cast over-the-top illusions. Y'know things Fae's are good at."

He tossed a canteen at her, "You don't need to have *Undine, Sylph*, and *Phantasy-Ars* like me."

"Ugh, I just *had* to be born now. Those darn *Droughts* ruined everything."

"Trust me, Sprout, the *Droughts* were an excellent thing. Magic from that era is too powerful. Lumenopal and Grimoires are better options.

"Says the Fae who trained with Dwarves and talking Biyrds to learn to change their *Flux* to channel an incompatible Od." She pouted. "How else am I supposed to slay a *Gallu*-Dragon or *Gallu*-Therian?"

"Bah! Some of my best comrades were Arcane wielders, and they faired just well with *Analeptic* and *Synergist-Ars*. So will you!"

He laughed as he stroked his beard and placed his hand on his knife. Anemone saw that he had a habit of touching that sword-breaker of his every time he thought about the past. Yet again, Spriggan began to tell old tales of yore, and his stories were as old as his gray wooly beard and brows. She smiled back at him, but Anemone's inability to use *Sylph* Od to create wind-based Ars was a sore spot for her. It seemed that Anemone's *Flux* left her unable to channel any elemental Od. Luckily, Anemone could still conduct the mysterious Od, *Arcane*. He had fought alongside many connected to the Arcane Od. They could use magic like Phantasy-Ars for illusions, Analeptic-Ars for healing, Saboteur-Ars to undermine foes, and Synergist-Ars to bolster themselves or allies.

"We didn't have Lumenopal and Grimoires when I was younger. So those whose Flux couldn't use Od had no chance to cast Ars. You, on the other hand, still have Arcane."

"And I'm still an Od—"

Anemone stopped before speaking, not wanting to talk about a word she hated hearing. It was a social taboo she didn't want to have by her people's standards. Being unable to caste *Sylph-Ars* practically made her one by default.

"I know I'm being selfish, but it's still infuriating. Lumenopal helps, but *Od* conversion takes twice the effort!"

"Effort is fundamental! It keeps you humble."

Spriggan pointed at his bejeweled eyepatch and a scar beneath his uniform.

"Without humility, you'll lose more than you know. Need I tell you how I got *that* scar!"

"No, it's fine—"

He tore open his coat to reveal a wicked scar the size of a fist across his chest. Anemone turned her head to the side, only gazing at it from the corner of her eyes.

"Back when your grandparents Dagda and Medb were ruling, a coup d'etat had occurred inside Tir-noNog's walls. The lands of Abhainn-Reatha were far more lawless...."

"I already know Spriggan. Magic, Od, and Celestials were everywhere, just like freedom, death, and glory."

"Aos-Si fought tooth and nail to survive each other. This was a time when Denizens still roamed the lands. There was magic beyond the Fifth tier that could lay waste to whole lands."

He was already ignoring her and continuing his drawn-out story. Spriggan had a habit of removing his tunic and pointing to the scars etched into his old yet lean body with every tale entailed. He often reminisced about resource wars against rival Aos-Si kingdoms. Serving under Queen Medb as a youth, he fought before the Pylon Droughts. It was when Aos-Si of all kinds wandered Abhainn-Reatha freely, long before Aos-Si kind established their kingdoms.

Before the Pylon Droughts, many performed magic without Lumenopal stones and Grimoires. When the Pylon Droughts happened, everyone lost the ability to use Ars above the Fifth tier. The closest they had ever come to it was theories of an old-world Ars capable of burning away the presence of a *Gallu-Utukku*. Only the Denizens knew of such knowledge; they were beings gone to the annals of time. As Spriggan said, "Old-world magic is too dangerous," Anemone felt it gave everyone a better chance to defend themselves.

"I wonder what type of Ars the Denizens use? Do you think it could stop the *Gallu*?"

She had mumbled those words aloud, not expecting Spriggan to hear her, but he stopped his story and nodded.

"No Sprout. Aos-Si kind is far too turbulent for such knowledge."

"Why say that? The *Gallu-Utukku* terrorizes everyone, including Therianthropes. That makes no sense."

"You're young, Sprout. You haven't seen the world as I have. As bad as it seems, the world is balanced. As one dies, another is born."

"There you go again... Don't Aos-Si have the right to better lives? How is everything balanced when so many have their lives taken?"

"I've already explained myself dozen times. You'll only understand once you see the world for yourself."

"You and your worldly views always stump me. Knowing Titania, I doubt I'll even see past the Wildlands."

Spriggan always had this peculiar part of him she could never understand. Od slowly fading away, even Grimoires seemed to be losing their edge. The best option was to retrieve more shards of a stone found mainly in the Wildlands, Lumenopal. They were crystals comprised of pure Od found far past the Arid Sea in the Wildlands. Nowadays, only foolhardy souls would dare venture into such a place. Tales of yore spoke of when everything past the Southern region was still lush and open for exploration. Stories told of a land beyond the Wildlands abundant in Lumenopal and Pylons. Now everyone lay behind walls for protection, with only scouts and fools foolhardy enough to explore desolate lands. Almost everyone relied on Lumenopal stones for more than Ars, and many still believe it was our best option.

No one knew what caused the Droughts, but everyone knew its effects. When the Od in the air began to thin suddenly, casting any superior magical Ars that could bring down a mountain or drench lands became challenging. What took one well-skilled individual to launch such an Ars now took ten of hundreds to pull off. As time passed, fewer Aos-Si of each generation was born, unable to cast magic.

"Spriggan?" Anemone called out to him. "Do you think an *Od-less* can beat a Therian?"

Word stopped coming out of Spriggan's mouth as he pulled out his flask to take a sip. As he closed his flask and tossed it at her, Spriggan laid his eye on Anemone. He sat with a long stare and wiped his long-bearded face as his head nodded.

"Who called you an *Od-less*?" He said sternly.

"Does it matter who said it?" She clenched the flask. "Everyone believes having only Arcane is just one step away from being *Od-less*."

He shook his head. "These kids these days don't know. I had comrades who forsaken their natural Od affinity to specialize in Analeptic-Ars healing. Doesn't the academy honor support classes?"

"Yeah, but even some of the professors belittle it. Synergist-Ars may have been the foundation to Apothecary-Ars, but the convenience of making healing tonics and elixirs is less taxing—"

"Bah!" Spriggan interrupted. "You listen to me, Sprout! When you're out of all those materials and tonics, all you have is your wit and brawn! I've seen Fae cast only Exceed to outspeed a Dragon or Gladius outwrestle a Minotaur. Forget that Apothecary farce!"

He ended that sentence with a smile and signaled that she takes a swig. She smiled and took a mouth full. Instantly her face furrowed at its peculiar blend of sweet spice and dry. It was another one of his homemade brews. This one blended Seritona, Betula, Anisum, and fermented Pyrus fruit with honey. The mixture was suspiciously too sweet, but she could see his hard work paying off.

Anemone tossed it back at him after a few more mouthfuls knowing she'd drank too much. He laughed; oddly, the less she trusted it, the closer he was to the blend he wanted. She never understood why he was insistent on brewing this particular flavor, but it had been his project for quite some time. Often, she joined him in collecting the herbs he needed for all his brewing needs, but her reaction was always the same for this particular blend. That flavor almost made her forget how uneasy she felt for a second.

Even though he tried to make her feel better being an *Od-less*, her chest tightened when that word echoed. Many deemed those without elemental Od less favorable than those without none. Traditional healing magic was being replaced by those who learned to synthesize ingredients with Od to make healing tonics and elixirs. Because of how little Od it expended, many found making them far more efficient than casting any *Synergist-Ars* or *Analeptic-Ars*. Anemone already felt that her skills would become a thing of the past in time.

Regardless of how she felt about the circumstances, she always held Spriggan's motivation and stories dear. Even if hearing Spriggan's stories of powerful Fae, who were far more skilled in Arcane-Ars, seldom put her at ease, her smiles never stopped during the stories of his allies. His arms flailed about as he described every moment, and his words were often humorous and entertaining, even if she could tell they were serious. The scars etched into Spriggan's body proved his battles were no laughing matter. Looking at her torn dress again, she couldn't help but think of her.

"Was Titan—" she paused. "—Mother ever afraid of Therians?"

"Your mother was always bold, even when she didn't swing a sword. She...."

There was an elongated phase in his sentence that Anemone noticed, and he closed his eyes and took a breath before he continued to speak. It was another habit she saw whenever he talked about Titania. For as long as she could remember, the two seemed estranged, only speaking when necessary. Spriggan and Titania crossing paths was only official business if it wasn't politics or about her.

"Therianthropes were just wild beasts called Therians back in my day. Times have changed; they've become far more adept and intelligent after ages of confrontation with our kin," his face furrowed.

"So, the books didn't lie. Aos-Si blood made them stronger."

"Aye, our flesh changed their bodies and gave a speech to them. They built homes and pillaged our lands and lives thanks to us. But the Ars they wield is nature's gift, necessary to keep us in check." He took another mouthful and pointed at her.

"If they ever asked this on the Accolade Trials, remember Dragons were already superior to Aos-Si in every way... Except what?"

"Gestation. Aos-Si outclasses Dragons in numbers and birth rates."

"Good!" he nodded. "And what do we need them for?"

"Their yolk, to breed lesser dragons, and their shells make great anti-Od armor."

"You might be just ready for those Trials, Sprout!" Spriggan stroked his chin, "Just thinking about it reminds me of the old days with Quarz and Rellzy. A single Dragon egg could feed a band of twenty warriors, and by the time you got your hands on it, you only had to feed five. I wonder if Quarz still has that Dragonkin around?"

Spriggan brought up one of his old stories she had heard before. It was about his comrades sneaking into one of the nesting grounds for wild Vulcan Dragons. They could not catch any hatchlings, but they had gotten their hands on some eggshells. That was an absolute victory, as the Dragons had complete control over Od, just like Aos-Si did. However, their Ars were far more potent than the average Aos-Si and nearly resembled old-world magic. Much like Therianthropes eating Aos-Si, Dragons had also gained the ability to talk and shift into Aos-Si-like figures from eating them.

As powerful as they were, Dragon mating periods occurring once every score and gestation cycles lasting up to five years, infant loss was detrimental to their kind. Although adult dragons were fearsome, their long juvenile stages and birth cycles were vulnerable. Their yolk's nutrients and their eggshell's elemental resistance made them a prize. Keeping dragons as pets also made them an essential tool to many Aos-Si or Therianthropes. Ultimately, Therianthropes and Aos-Si outnumbering them proved to be an effective method of keeping them under control.

Spriggan talked about his adventures and made Anemone dwell on how prepared she was for the Trials ahead. Anemone suddenly remembered how hectic life was about to become for her. Although she welcomed it, horrors were waiting to challenge her. Suddenly her focus was ruined by Spriggan prodding the butt of his scepter into her forehead.

"Are you still listening?" He poked.

"Sorry, Spriggan," she apologized as she yawned. "I've been tired as of late."

His displeased face shifted. "Are you still having those dreams that—?" His words stopped abruptly.

Anemone raised her brow in confusion, "What are you—?" The sound of bells ringing erratic caught her ear.

"The *Furin Bells*!" He hopped to his feet.

A sudden burst of air forced Anemone's eyes shut, and when she opened them, Spriggan was already gone. She slapped her face to get her head focused and chased after the sound. It was a different set of bells than they had just checked that sounded. Anemone could feel her heart pounding in her throat as she got closer. The sweat from her palm kept her sleeves wet even as the wind rushed by her. She kept wiping her forehead and did her best to watch her breathing. It was one thing Spriggan consistently reinforced during moments of peak stress.

A wretched odor punched her nostrils as she stuck to the upper canopy. An intense mix of dried soil, fecal matter, and old sweat easily rivaled a Minotaur's musk. Soon after, the sound of wheels creaking through the loose soil of the forest floor caught her attention. A group of six Therianthropes Minotaur pulled sets of narrow prison-like caravans below. It was also the first time Anemone had seen Minotaurs outside her textbooks. Their arms were as thick as Greater Elm Tree trunks, and they easily towered over the locked-up Dwarves. Two of them had Lumenopal shards jutting out of their bodies, and Anemone could tell what element they could use. One had the Ruby-red Cinnabar Lumenopal, the stone that harnessed the flames of Vulcan, and the other had the yellow Topaz Lumenopal of the earthbound Oread.

The wooden walls of the caravan were as thick as the trees surrounding them. Locked behind its pillar-sized metal bars, a mix of Aos-Si stuffed it to the brim. Fae and Elves continuously nudged each other as they fought for breathing room and held their noses. A few of them had clothes that still looked a bit fresh. While others only had torn garbs and dirt covering their exposed bodies. Anemone noticed the smell was from them and the Minotaurs who plucked them from their home.

The look in the eyes of the other Aos-Si in either torn clothes or naked was vacant. Not even the light that peered through the forest openings reflected in them. The ones in fresher clothes still had far more grit left in them. They hollered and slammed their reddened fist against the solid metal bars. What stuck out most was the sight of

Dwarves amongst the group. The two looked far more uncomfortable than the rest; seeing them out and about was rare. Being almost seven feet tall, they stuck out from other Aos-Si, who barely reached six feet. One of them was missing a leg and had a large black marking across his face. The other was a female who did her best to keep his leg bound, but the space there made it hard for her to tighten the knot properly.

A Minotaur's sudden roar forced Anemone's focus back onto the hulking beasts. Anemone's eyes notice that the Minotaur with Cinnabar Lumenopal had bellowed so ghastly. A young elven male from inside the cage had stabbed the Cinnabar Minotaur. The blade lodged inside the Minotaur's abdomen instantly clenched and crushed the Elf's arm. Its roaring muted the painful screams of the Elf he held. Immediately the Minotaur snapped the Elf's arm off and reached through the cage's bars. Its broadened forearm bent the metal aside like loose tree branches. Clenching the Elf's head, his hand enveloped in flames, crushing its skull as it cracked like stale bread. As far as Anemone was, the smell of charred flesh flew past her. She could hear the other Aos-Si frenzy from the scalding flesh splashed on them. The Minotaur with Topaz Lumenopal roared and silenced them right after he slapped the head of the Cinnabar Minotaur.

When he unlocked the cage, he flung the lifeless Elf's body into the air with no remorse. The limp body disappeared as its blood and limbs scattered over the forest floor. Anemone could barely hold back her gasp, almost escaping her mouth as the Elf's blood-drenched something invisible, a long jaw. As the beast crunched on the Elf's body, special marks began to glow along its fairly transparent body. Its blood allowed Anemone to faintly see the shape of its dagger-sized teeth and skull.

Anemone couldn't look away nor cancel out the sound of a body snapping like twigs. The obscure markings on its body let Anemone realize what was before her. Anemone's blood went cold as she grew more horrified. When a hand suddenly touched her shoulder from behind, she instinctively jumped back, pulling out her blade. Spriggan had deflected the strike as his sight stayed locked on what unfolded below.

"I'm glad you didn't avert your eyes from that *Gallu-Utukku*," he whispered. "After the Accolade Trials, you'll have to be prepared for the things even dragons can fear."

Spriggan kept his hand on her back for a second before spreading his wings and flying away. After wiping her mouth, she followed. The fear of the *Gallu-Utukku* was drilled into her head many times. They had arrived from beyond the stars. Everyone feared them; even dragons stood little chance against them. Their arrival had caused a significant toll on everyone's population. It was capable of parasitism, but no one knew what it wanted. All they knew was anything overtaken by a *Gallu-Utukku* became a rage-induced creature that was several times harder to kill than its regular counterparts. It overhauled a creature's mind and body and forced it to do whatever it pleased. No one had ever killed one; they only caused it to find another host or ornament to possess.

Knowing that this was only the first of many sights she would witness, Anemone clenched her arm to the point her nails pierced her skin. For her to personally experience a *Gallu's* presence continually sent shivers through her body. The sight of how easy that *Gallu* dismembered the Elf's body fixated in her mind. It made her realize how underprepared she was. That doubt made her question if she was ready for tomorrow's Accolade Trials.

She would often visualize herself in battle, casting over-the-top Ars or spells decimating hordes of *Gallu-Utukku*. They would be victorious despite the odds against her and her soon-to-be team. After seeing this, changing her mind was an excellent idea. However, she couldn't forgive herself for feeling so cowardly. The sight was so upsetting that her body wanted to heave. If she had eaten something this morning, she might have. Instead, they were just dry heaves. Even with conflict on the decline, things like this were daily outside Tir-noNog, but never this close. With this incident close to home, she feared Tir-noNog's safety. She feared she wouldn't be strong enough to protect her home or herself. If it wasn't for Tir-noNog's barrier, Anemone knew their kingdom might have been at risk long ago. She knew none of this would still stand if it weren't for her mother.

...Tir-noNog and the Four Winds

It had taken her quite a bit, but the light from the forest clearing shined in her eyes. At last, she was home. The sight warmed her heart, and she felt slightly better. In the distance, more giant trees stretched into the sky and had lights glowing within them and around their branches. Fae had begun to turn on the lights of their tree-carved homes before the sun fell. It showed Anemone that she had made it back in time. While the sun was still up, getting through the barrier was easy for marked residents.

She hopped past the Fifth district with speed and quickly entered the First District. When she reached the First District, a grand woven tapestry of Titania hung across two trees caught her eye. It was in front of one of the major libraries of the kingdom. She gazed across it and saw the story of her mother leading the Fae to Tir-noNog and settling in this very spot. Anemone could see someone giving a tour to some travelers, and as they spoke, she clenched her arm and turned away.

Tribal flags of all Fae hung from tree to tree across the skies, and the roads below filled with more than just Fae, Elves, and the occasional Gnome. Demi-Aos-Si with scaly skin, like the Dragonkin or the snake-bodied Lamia, roamed through, with the gill having Pisces. Even the grey-skinned Goblins and miniature-statured Brownies were walking around. Tir-noNog was a melting pot for Aos-Si but seeing this much Herpenton and Merfolk was irregular.

Stalls of all kinds of Aos-Si Herpenton and Merfolk cultures stood on the side of the roads. Voices calling out from left to right hollered to grab the attention of onlookers. The children were either running through the Bazar or sitting near the theater square listening to a storyteller's embellished stories of Tir-noNog's history. As she looked around, noticing the seasonal décor of simple colored flags representing an element of Sylph, Undine, Oread, and Vulcan, she knew what day it was.

"I can't believe I forgot about the Four Winds Festiva," she thought.

The sounds of the festivities and her rumbling stomach hushed her words. Fanfare echoed through the roads, and the smell of unfamiliar foods arose; her mouth watered. Although she had forgotten, Fae had begun celebrating the Festival of Four Winds yesterday. Tir-noNog celebrated Fae culture, unity, and their yielding perseverance every year. Anemone stood for a moment and remembered her tutors telling her the fable of the Western winds. They had followed the winds that blew the seeds of Arbor-folk in their incredible migration and soon found this land filled with life and food.

After that, the Eastern winds brought forth a "great freeze" that cooled the grounds and brought life to a near halt as it raged for years. She could hear Elders reminisce and drone on how worldly and life conflicts mirrored the season even in the background. Many told scary winter stories during the festival to reinforce Fae's gratitude for living in prosperous times. *Everything was cyclical, and nothing was new.* As she continued to walk through the plaza, she heard another guide explaining the symbolism of its celebration.

"It took five years to create the treaty with Albion and another five to unite each of the Four Great Fae kingdoms under Tir-noNog. None of this would be possible if it weren't for her majesty."

"That's not true! A'ma says if it weren't for Vestri's sacrifice, Tir-noNog would be gone!"

A young child spoke from the crowd, but everyone ignored their words. The tour guide continued about more of Titania's success and the glory of Tir-noNog.

"In the queen's words, '*We must remember the past is a window to see what we must learn.*' Just as Titania learned from her mother, Queen Medb, who united the Fae."

A scowl grew across Anemone's face as she saw the guide point at a large carving of Titania and the preceding royalty. All of her words went in one ear and out the other. Anemone knew much of the king's sacrifice, and as Titania might say, "It was a necessary sacrifice to uphold order." As those words crossed her mind, Anemone quickly walked off, instantly placing her hand over her mouth. The feeling of a storm brewing in her stomach returned as that elf popped into her head again.

Quickly she stumbled near a waste bin and dry heaved again. Coughs continued even when nothing came out. Besides wanting to rush down there, she knew she wasn't strong enough. Even if she was bold enough for such a task, there was no telling how helpful she could have been. Her eyes watered as she silently cursed herself. Under the sound of her coughs, she heard voices chattering in the background.

"Wow, she can't handle her liquor like the Queen."

"Right? Are we sure that "Od-less" is Titania's child?"

"Yeah, there's no way she's ready for the Trials."

"The Trials? Forget her! Do you think we are? Haven't you heard?"

"Please, those rumors are baseless. Any comrade-at-arms with half a brain can complete that test and those random tasks."

"Not the test, you idiot!" Their voice hushed before they spoke again. "I heard *Remnants* are lurking in the woods."

As she turned her head, that pair of Fae walked by, whispering to the point the crowded streets drowned out their words. Anemone scoffed as she wiped her face mocking their lips with her hand.

"Titania this, Titania that...everyone loves her coattail, but I'll show them. I'll be just as great!"

After taking a deep breath, Anemone placed her hands on her hip, hoping to command a presence for herself. Not a moment soon, she found her face hung back over the trash can. She stood up and straightened herself out one more time before looking for Spriggan.

"Holy Celestials, I hate liquor." She thought.

The opportunity to prove her skills to herself, Titania, and others had arrived. The festival always occurred right before the Accolade Trials, and Anemone was finally of age and rank. After passing the Accolade Trials, she knew her post was outside Tir-noNog's walls. The more she thought about that elf, the more she wanted to prevent such atrocities from happening again.

When she found Spriggan, he talked to an Arbor-Magna Provincial Commander. After Anemone saw the large scar on his left face, she knew who it was. Commander Airelle was a Fae commander infamous among cadets for his bold attitude. His uniform was sharp and neat, like his low-cut hair. Even with the stitches woven across parts of his uniform's shoulder and spine, you could see his stiff nature.

Contrary to most Fae with somewhat androgynous features, he looked as tough as Spriggan. His scarred eye scared any youth who stared into it. It didn't help that when he caught you looking into his glare, it felt like a trick question to ask, "How did he get it?" Every time someone did, he had them run drills until they passed out. He claimed that his drills were a preventative medicine that would prevent such a thing from befalling them if they worked hard enough.

As far as Anemone knew, they had an interesting dynamic. Spriggan claimed they had known each other back in their heydays, but it didn't feel like it. There was always thick air around when they talked, and she wasn't the only one who noticed. He never told her not to worry about it, but Airelle often had it out for Anemone. She was one of his favorite targets for surprise drills and questions. He never let her live it down when she joined the Academy later than everyone else.

Instantly, she stood back, avoiding his line of sight as he and Spriggan discussed the group of Therianthropes nearby. She overheard Spriggan tell Commander Airelle to ensure there weren't any long-distance observers within a twenty-flight radius. If she knew one thing about Airelle, he was thorough and precise.

"With a new moon only a few days away, there's a chance those flying Blood-suckers are close to peak strength," Airelle huffed.

"Well, would you rather deal with Chiropterans or Lycanthropes snooping around our woods?"

"Neither. Both those opportunistic fiends would prey on our troops in a second. Especially those Hounds! At least Minotaurs are all brawn."

"You're one to talk, Rellzy. Maybe we'll have ourselves another *Blue crescent*," Spriggan said.

Commander Airelle hissed as he turned and talked to one of the knights next to him. Even if she didn't want to ever run into either of them, some of her still wanted to know how she would fare against them. She knew Chiropterans weren't all that strong and practically blind, but their long fleshy wings allowed them to fly swiftly and outmaneuver even the most adept Fae in the trees. With their long-shaped ears, they could hear sounds at a distance that skilled Aos-Si could only dream of having. Not to mention they emitted high-pitched sounds that melted your mind.

Lycanthropes had hearings half as great as Chiropterans, but their sense of smell and powerful claws more than made up for it. They were common threats to the barrier, especially under a new or full moon. No one wanted anything as significant as a group of Minotaur or *Gallu-Utukku* finding the wall. Once they did and rallied together, Anemone knew it would be a long battle.

Anemone knew she hadn't even hunted an Insecta, yet the two warriors before her had hunted creatures five times their size. Sooner or later, she would have to do more if she ever hoped to fight a Minotaur. While Spriggan and the Commander continued their discussion, Anemone's eyes wandered into the distance catching the sight of Acaulis. He was draped in Celadon and Cinnabar Lumenopal shards from his crown to the rings on his fingers. His attire was befitting of being Albion's second Elven prince. Her eyes were so focused on him that she didn't notice Spriggan had finished his conversation with Airelle and stood next to her.

"Don't start trouble with other royals. At least, not yet."

"Yet?" Anemone questioned. "What do you mean?"

"Acaulis is also participating in the Accolade Trials. Though, I recommend not fighting him. He is Genni's son."

"Don't worry, I won't...unless it's a part of my directive," she smirked. "Besides, Acaulis is King Gentiana's child. He's 'Royal'd and Spoil'd,' and he can't fight, unlike me."

Spriggan could only shake his head, knowing she would be looking for an excuse to fight him. She ignored him and kept her attention on Acaulis. Acaulis often avoided anything that didn't affect the kingdom of Albion and seldom mingled with anyone who wasn't an Elf. Whatever the reason, she knew it probably involved his father. Anemone found the sight of Acaulis speaking to a non-Albion Elf unexpected. It was so peculiar that she noticed it also caught Spriggan's eye. Especially since the stranger, he was talking to was an Aos-Si wearing a Tir-noNog uniform.

"Do you know the lad the prince just crossed paths with? The one with the bindings over his eyes," Spriggan asked.

Anemone could see that the curled brown-haired fellow was also a companion-at-arms. It took a second for her to see his face, but she recognized him when he faced them. Thanks to the purple patch on his uniform's epaulet and the black veil over his eyes, she realized he was from Albion. All military trainees were required to wear Tir-noNog's uniforms, but the color of one of their epaulets was for their home kingdom, and the other was golden for Tir-noNog.

"Ugh, it's Rubus, one of the few weirdos to cover his eyes like that. He was in both my Strategies class and lower-division mock combat."

"So, he is a Dökkálfar," Spriggan murmured. "Are there any males your age you don't want to fight?" he continued.

"There's technically Aron, but Y'know...Most of my peers don't approve of me."

"Well, Fae still ostracizes as much as elves do."

"No wings, no *Sylph-Ars*, and I show up late in the academy. Blame Titania for giving me this hand of cards," Anemone scorned.

"You're too hard on her."

"I know, *great* Queen, tough mom."

"I wish you two would get along already— Just make sure you grab the Grimoire before you do anything else. And for the love of Lauma, don't forget to change your dress."

Spriggan sighed and told her to find Quarz to obtain her Grimoire before separating. He was a traveler who knew Spriggan from his heydays and owed him a favor. As much as she wanted Spriggan to go with her, he had to find the caravan they had seen earlier. Judging by the urgency Airelle had on his face talking to another Commander, Anemone knew they were scavenging for a few more troops. Some of her wanted him to ask if she could follow him back to the caravan, but she stopped. Instead, Anemone waved weakly and stared at Spriggan's back as they headed off.

It took her a moment before she could force herself through the bazaar's main road as he left. He did not bother asking her if she wanted to go with him, which gave her an answer she already knew. She kept her arms folded the whole time, recalling her training. Even after training for eight years, that haunting scene continuously found a way to creep into her mind. Anemone could feel her eyes swell with tears, and she refused to let that feeling go any deeper. Now she was alone with her thoughts.

Anemone understood she was lucky to see Spriggan constantly return from his patrols but worried about what it would be like if he didn't come back every time he left. Or if he was gone as long as Titania usually was. So much was on her mind she wanted to ignore it all.

While walking, a ball abruptly slaps Anemone into the side of her head. She turned and saw Aos-Si children playing with a Dragonkin group.

"If it's one thing I'll give Titania credit for, it's the sight of Demies and Aos-Si having some peace."

The Demi-Dragonkin had scales protruding along their skin and abnormally strong-looking teeth. They were a hybrid between a Dragon and an Aos-Si. To her, this was always heartwarming to see Demi-hybrids playing alongside pureblooded Aos-Si. It was a sight she heard was only possible here in Tir-noNog. Other places were far more homogenous, with a small mix of segregated Aos-Si. Tir-noNog was one of the few places where multiple cultures thrived together. After rubbing her head, Anemone feigned being scared and chased the kids. Although she could hear voices and chatter in the background, she couldn't care less, and neither did most kids. Sadly, it wouldn't take long for an old Elven parent to grab their child as they spoke under their breath.

"Don't fraternize with those Dragon-kin and Fae...They'll turn on you!"

"But the princess—?"

"That Wingless Princess will curse yer Od, just like she did the Queen. You'll be without Ars! An Od-less unable to help our family!"

When Anemone turned to the crowd, she could hear murmuring among them. All of their eyes stared daggers into her. It was the same scowl they always wore when someone didn't belong. She didn't even need to listen to what they had to say to know she was in the wrong. Her smile was faint; clenching her right arm, she decided to wave goodbye to the Dragonkin and the Fae children, who continued to play. Even as she took in the sights and sounds of the festival, everything almost seemed muted. The bustling of the crowd started to tune out, and everyone seemed blurred.

Fae had to play it nicely in public regardless of how they felt. Being a soldier in the Arbor Magna and royalty meant no one could outright disrespect her, but she was still the runt of her kind who cursed their *"Savior"* queen. No matter how often she heard words like that, she still hearted them. Anemone bowed her head and walked off.

Her eye drifted to a performance in the distance on a stage made in the central plaza. She vaguely remembered that event, only recalling that it was her job to perform a ceremonial dance in front of everyone. Even if it was a dance she had no interest in, she abided, knowing Titania would be there to see it. Anemone could remember the excitement in her chest as she thought about seeing Titania in the crowd as she performed. That feeling had disappeared when Titania was nowhere to be seen. After that, her memories from that night were vague, practically word of mouth.

Anemone slapped her cheeks and focused on the streets paved with Sylph-like décor. Her eyes watched all kinds of stands filled with food and trinkets. There were wind fish, feathers, gale cutouts, and tons of banners showing the other beings known for controlling Sylph Od. Along with other tribal flags, decorations hung from the trees that sprouted from most of the mud buildings in Tir-noNog. At one of the stalls, she saw beautiful necklaces of black feathers and Sylph Lumenopal sold by Tengu Avians. It was her first time seeing one in their Avian form and Aos-Si veil. Both had robust dark feathered wings as broad as her arms and thick talon-like feet, but the one in the Aos-Si form had an upper body and face that looked as normal as hers. She had heard they had Ars, just like the Dragons, to mold their body into the shapes of Aos-Si, but it was terrific.

"Hurry-hurry, KAW! If you need something to put the wind under your feathers, we Tengu have it all, KAW!"

The stall beside them had some Merfolk who kept their webbed feet and glossed scales soaked in water. Many lined up for their pearls and conches that manipulated Undine Od. She could hear them shouting out their sales pitch as well.

"You won't just hear the ocean; you'll feel it! And shoot it!"

Before Anemone took another step, the overwhelming blend of spices, meats, and salt smacked her. The smells forced her mouth to water, but there were too many options roasted Gryllidea Insecta, crushed Mori, or maybe some elven or Gnome delicacies. Unlike Fae, who are big on eating Insecta, Gnome and Elves preferred eating other animals, such as fish like Griphognathus or wild beasts like the large-headed Entelodont and great-horned Megaloceros. She wasn't used to those meats, so they upset her stomach. If anything, an Elven vegetarian dish might work as well. Knowing that she would run into either Aron or Aronia, she held off on food as last-minute prep for the Accolade trials was far more imperative.

After the last part of the written exam, she'd be out in the wilds for the practical part of the Accolade trials. There was no need to buy any armor since their uniform would be sturdy and light. Instead, she decided to grab some Lumenopal jewelry to prepare for tomorrow. She planned to carry a bow, dirks, a sword, and a shield into the field. As she walked through, some lovely knives to buy caught her eye. Her head turned as her legs kept forward since she already had five pairs.

As much as she wanted to, she knew it was an excellent idea to save up her well-earned Aegis and Aurum. She even saw beautiful Rubies and Emeralds across multiple stands that caught her eye, but she needed Lumenopal stones. It wouldn't be easy to find anything significant for a staff or a Grimoire, but a simple necklace or armlet enhances her *Flux* to absorb more Arcane Od would do. Soon, a stall with the perfect Lumenopal earrings appeared after walking around longer.

"How much for the Arcane earrings?

The Goblins figured he could trick her from the look on his face. He scratched his neck with shrugging shoulders, "250 Aegis or 125 Aurums."

Anemone's shoulders drooped at the Goblin's statement.

"That was double the price from last year!"

"Surry boot times are hard. Even with da merchant discount, da increased toll hurts. Titania's been kind, but that Gentiana hasn't."

"I thought military discounts were still enforced. I guess even Albion has it rough."

"I see the Armada keeps their foot soldiers in da dark too. Haven't you heard?"

Anemone's brows furrowed, "No. I haven't."

He signaled her to get closer. "Da South is practically dry now... Finfinne is the only viable mining region for Lumenopal Pylons. Gentiana's grip is in full swing now."

"At least I'll have more reason to leave the kingdom now," she sighed.

Anemone's haggling was as proficient as a cobblestone smashing a hammer; she could only sigh. Droughts aside, finding Lumenopal inland wasn't that easy either. Outside of Arbor Magna military rations, raiding a Pylon deposit filled with Lumenopal somewhere out in Southern Oryza was possible but unlikely. Southern Oryza was now particularly scarce with Lumenopal. Most of the Lumenopal shipments came from expeditions further south of the Finfinne region.

Finfinne was far south of Tir-noNog and Albion, past the Oryza Wildlands and next to the Arid Sea, the natural border separating the Southern and Northern Hemispheres. Since tariffs were high and expensive to bring from the South, she knew the merchant wasn't lying. Albion had just gotten through its reconstruction period, and King Gentiana controlled its surplus. The high tariff percentages only added to Tir-noNog's shortages.

Upon closer inspection, she could see some of his inventory was fractured. Even as a novice, she could tell by their shape that someone had chipped them from a larger stone. Messing with damaged Lumenopal wasn't safe for any projectile Ars. It was common for misfires to occur in life-or-death situations. On the other hand, it wasn't that bad for arrow tips and Synergist or some Saboteur Ars.

Since one wouldn't be drawing a vast amount of external Od into it, it wouldn't conflict too much with your *Flux*. Still, the stone was likely to crack faster and blow up in your face.

Anemone depended on Aronia or Aron for times like this, as they would have quickly cleared this merchant's ego. Anemone's body shifted from the added weight of someone leaning on her shoulder. With a Malus fruit in her hand, Aronia had appeared out of the blue. You could see the vendor's eyes go from her head down to her chest. Aronia's stature was vase-like and toned to the tee. Being far taller than Anemone, she was too big to be leaning on her like furniture. Anemone was always mildly jealous of Aronia and felt the Celestials had to have personally crafted her from high-grade Bronze.

"Speak of the *Gallu*, and they'll wander to you," Anemone snickered.

"It's likelie da fact Ye look like a damn boot yer gettin' played," Aronia murmured.

She wrapped her arms around Aronia and playfully pleaded. "Nia!!! Please DOO Sumthin."

"Geez yer whiney, quit yer gantin' this is without a doubt some swickery. There's a merch not too far, selling the same thin fer 225ag."

"What!?! Where?" Anemone gasped.

"Impossible!!!" the merchant yelled.

"Ye, betcha." Aronia unbuttoned her shirt and reached into her bosom to pull out her necklace as she leaned over. "I got this here necklace fer 210Ag, and I bet those would go nice with this," she continued.

The merchant's eyes rolled upward. "I'll give it to ya for 220Ag. Yoo, don't have to go all the way over there."

"That's not bad," she replied, straightening her posture, "but if you're willing to drop it. I'm sure—"

"No, no... I'll do it for the 200," he said with defeat. Quickly he changed his mind, "No! I mean—!"

"Sold! Merchant's code! Ye, can't change a verbal agreement on yer price!"

"Damn... Fine, you drive a hard bargain." The merchant tossed up the earrings, and Aronia caught them.

They walk off giggling, and Anemone wraps her arms around Aronia, kissing her on the cheek. "I ever tell you how much I love you."

"Oh, quit yer pandering. I'm sure all yer yaldi ta me's why lads dinnae approach me."

"I thought all a succubus wanted was to be loved."

"Hochmagandy and Lov are two different snashters, Luv. But both are good," Aronia humorously scoffed as she buttoned her blouse up. "Gettin' that Grimoire for the grand TirNog Armada?"

"Yup, it's registered. Now I don't have to worry about the Phloem Guard or other Arbor Magna jailing me."

"Abusing royal authority, aye?" She laughed.

After some banter and indulging in festival meals, they made their way to the Quarz's shop.

...Power People Pages

As the two continued towards Quarz's shop, they came across a rowdy crowd in the middle of the walkway. The group was roaring and cheering as if they were observing a spectacle. Anemone and Aronia looked at each other and assumed it was a historical demonstration. Both weren't interested in another history lesson since they had already done the historical qualifier to get approved for the Accolade Trials. They had already passed the central square near the library since everyone would observe Tir-noNog's founding story and the fall of the first Kingdom there.

Swimming their way through the ocean-like crowd, they saw Rubus and a group of Albionian Elves in the center. Rubus' face looked like it had taken quite a few blows while the Albionian stood slightly roughed up. As they got closer, one of the Elven Aos-Si started yelling at Rubus. Anemone couldn't identify who it was, but the only words that caught her mind were "filthy Dökkálfar." Dökkálfar was an uncommon word to Fae, but it was vernacular for Elven, "*Unseelie*."

As far as Anemone was concerned, the only noticeable difference between Dökkálfar and the Ljósálfar was their darkened sclera. If it wasn't because they all wore a veil covering their eyes, they might not even stick out. With this in mind, Anemone realized it was the first time she had seen Rubus's eyes. She understood how their sclera, as dark as the night sky, would strike fear into anyone who looked at them. However, Anemone didn't feel that way.

After all, both Aronia's parents and Spriggan had black sclera, and none of them were evil in her eyes. Then again, most would never know they were Unseelie since all of them could change the color of their sclera through sheer willpower. Besides their eyes, symbols often appear on their body or under their eyes during intense emotions. The more she thought about it, the more she couldn't recall either of those cases with Rubus.

"So much for the Treaty of Three Thrones, aye?" Aronia jeered.

"Good old-fashioned paper treaty. I guess ten years isn't long enough for Aos-Si," Anemone huffed

"Can ye blame them? All that bad blood is thick after non-stop centuries of war between us."

The *Treaty of Three Thrones* was a cease-fire between three major Aos-Si kingdoms: The Elven Kingdom of Albion in northern Abhainn-Reatha, The Fae Kingdom Tir-noNog, and The Western Dwarven Kingdom of Vestri. It was one of Titania's most outstanding achievements, but Anemone had mixed feelings. Anemone believed bloodshed and hatred should have disappeared, but Aos-Si lived too long. Most of those from that Era were old and alive. Even worse, many of them were too old to fight, and their children perished in their stead. All that remained were bitter elders and parentless children.

At the inner edge of the crowd, Anemone's eyes caught an Elf sent flying out of the epicenter. She had gotten so close that she saw an Elf holding Rubus back while another nailed him in the gut. Right before he punched Rubus in the face, Rubus head-butted the Elf behind him. Rubus had hit the Elf so hard it dazed him and loosened his grip. At that moment, Rubus moved his head to the side, causing the Elf in front to punch the one holding him. The force was so strong it sent that Elf to the ground. As he let go, Rubus grabbed the other Elf's arm flipping him over his shoulder and onto the floor. Soon after, the one launched out of the crowd rushed to rejoin the fight. Once Anemone noticed him trying to run back in, she tripped him, sending him flying into Rubus and the other Elves.

"By order of the Lauma Family Monarchy, I, Ninlil Anemone, order this senselessness to CEASE!" Anemone yelled.

The cheering immediately stopped, and everyone looked at Anemone where she stood. She held her chest high, strutting towards them with Aronia walking on her right side. They all stood up reluctantly as Rubus sat and looked at her straight.

"Didn't need the help, Wingless." Rubus stood up. "I had it covered."

"I wasn't doing it for you," she huffed. "This is a day of festivity and celebration. Leave your quarrels elsewhere!"

"One freak supporting another?" The head-butted one rebutted. "Sounds grand."

"Yeah, she's not even the Queen! She'd let us fight it out!"

"Ye, Elvies, do realize she's still royalty, right?"

Anemone's urge to shout boiled in her chest. Clenching her arm to focus on the pain brought her down for a moment, but she could feel her brow twitch. Even as she kept her face still, it wasn't easy to hear the crowd complain about her stopping the fight. Their words chipped at her demeanor like a sculptor picking at her rough edges. Unlike herself, Anemone knew Titania was far more battle-hardened and took pride in the friendly or frivolous battles. Anemone took a deep breath and closed her eyes, hoping to gather her thoughts.

Although she tried to stay calm, it got quickly ruined by someone in the background who called her a *Wingless killjoy*. Then another said, "This is why we don't like having Sh'fae around." Soon the rest started to scream, "LET THEM FIGHT!" in an uproar. After a few moments of their yelling, she shrugged her shoulders. Drawing her knife into the sky, she yelled at the top of her lungs.

"LET THEM FIGHT!"

The crowd went silent for a moment as they all stared at her. After a few seconds, one of the Albionian Elves sucker-punched Rubus sending him back to the ground. As the rest of them ganged up on him, the crowd cheered. Anemone put her blade away and walked off as Aronia stood back and looked at Rubus, getting his butt kicked just for a bit. A few moments later, Aronia ran up to Anemone and grabbed her shoulders.

"What was that about?"

"Well, Muspell, he said he had it covered."

"Wow, I expected ye to go all hero and defend the weak."

"I'll just leave it to the Phloem Guard or a Sargent to solve that issue. Besides, most of that crowd were other companions-at-arms. They're all probably on edge since tomorrow is the Accolade Trail's first part, and they probably have too much tension in their systems."

"Ah... trying to be caring in yer *own* way, aye? Real cheeky, aren't ye."

A silent huff of air left her lips after her shoulders slumped. As she went back through the crowd, they practically shoved her body around until she stumbled out. Not a moment later, she stood straight and walked off tall, ignoring the frenzy behind her. Anemone could not remember the last time she lashed out, much less caused trouble. Hearing them call Rubus a Dökkálfar made her feel sorry for him. If Anemone was honest, she didn't want to upset the crowd more than they were. The more she dwelled on it, the more it explained why he kept to himself and always kept his eyes hidden.

That fight was the first time she had ever looked at his body. His jacket was off, and she realized how smaller he looked without it. Rubus wasn't skinny, but he didn't look the type to take too many punches and come out on top. Although he had always gotten on her nerves, some of her wanted to protect him. As far as she was concerned, he had it covered. Her eyes looked at Aronia and then back to the crowd. Quickly she shook her head and kept moving forward.

"Nia, do you know anything about Rubus?" Her face grew flustered.

"No! I hardly know the lad! Why do ye ask?"

"Earlier today, I saw him with Acaulis, and now I see him getting into trouble."

"That's a surprise, Nin. You've never shown interest in someone before."

"No, it's not like that." Anemone nodded.

When Anemone turned around again, her eyes landed on Aronia, whose face said everything. Even still, Anemone didn't know what to think of her position. She didn't bother finishing her thought. However, she wasn't sure if she had one. Then a particular thought crossed her mind, "*If it were Titania, she might have a better solution.*" Once that thought set in, she no longer had the energy to deal with anything else. When it took only a few more minutes to find Quarz's shop, she forced a smile across her face. Her heart sprung some pep into her steps once she realized he had propped it up at the other end of the shopping district. It was a dingy carriage on sturdy old wheels with a Lesser-Drake at the helm, away from almost everyone. The cart looked like it had taken more of a beating than the oversized scaly lizard with scars across her body. Seeing one upfront felt terrific since Tir-noNog had always used brown Blattella Insecta or Emerald-winged Odonata for riding and Beatles for heavy pulls.

As they approached him, she saw he was having a minor disagreement with his Dragonkin assistant. Their discussion was somewhat calm, but Anemone overheard one of them mentioning *The Nectar*. The Dragonkin had a grim look on his face as he clenched the collar of Quarz' Gambeson. A sense of urgency in their discussion quickly faded when they noticed Anemone approaching. Before he left, they heard him tell Quarz, "To go as soon as possible." She and Aronia walked up to the Lesser-Drake and rubbed its snout, acting as if they heard nothing. The beast cooed as she stroked it.

"She's usually picky about who touches her. You must have your mother's tenderness."

"I doubt that," Anemone smiled. "Always heard compared to True Dragons, Lesser-Drakes were less intelligent but just as wild."

"Not true. The lack of speech capabilities is almost meaningless. Even though Lesser-Drakes are just as proud, they are far more docile."

The Elven man was dressed in a thick brown Gambeson with Rangifer hide boots. His long dark brown hair covered the scar on the whole left part of his face. Just like Spriggan, he had survived the ancient wars. When Quarz spoke, his voice sounded as gruff as his clothes looked. His face had a half-smile as he clenched a book in his hand. The look in his eyes was cold but full of life, just like Spriggan when he stared off. A few of their Academy Professors also looked like someone who had seen more lives lost than you could imagine. It was a look all youths feared but respected.

"Here you are, little miss," Quarz held the book out to her. "This one won't blow up in your hands. Don't get caught."

"Oh please, we all kno Nin doesn't want that tongin Titania would give her a before she gets lifted by the Armada. There's no way she'd get caught.

Anemone nodded as she took the book from his hands. Her eyes stayed locked on the Grimoire; Anemone was motionless. She didn't know how to act. Part of her was scared to death, knowing the consequences of owning an unlisted Grimoire. The other part was so excited that she couldn't hide the ear-to-ear grin on her face. Quarz continued to speak with as warm of a voice as his dry voice could muster as she stayed starstruck.

"That damned Cabinet of Nine embargo made bringing this thing a hassle."

"It feels strange holding this. The Arbor Magna wanted to find who was behind rigged Grimoires, yet here I am getting one for leisure."

"It's for the future ye want, not just fun and magic."

"I'm sure *he's* glad you received that. Just don't forget to sync your Od to that Grimoire."

"I'm surprised Spriggan was the organizer for this," Anemone agreed.

"At this point, Grimoires have replaced traditional Scribe-Casting. This will benefit you even if you don't see it yet. I see why Sprigg's has you focusing on conversion so much."

"You sound just like him."

"Oh Nin, quit actin' like the auldjin donnae kno what works. Sure, he's a wee scatterbrain, not dumb!"

"Although Od has become scarce, little miss CQC is a last resort. Trust me."

Anemone knew Quarz had a debt owed to Spriggan from their war days. She trusted Spriggan, but it blew her mind when he told her about the arrangements for Quarz to bring the Grimoire two years before the Grimoire Embargo. During that time, The Cabinet of Nine announced a memorandum to the public on Grimoires rigged to cast misfires. As part of the Grimoire Embargo, all residing Grimoires are registered in the Kingdom to reduce casualty chances. The laws sentenced anyone caught with an unregistered Grimoire to death. If they were lucky, they might stand trial. Even with that knowledge, Anemone held the Grimoire close to her chest and smiled, thanking Quarz.

"I still can't believe this."

Quarz smirked. "Agreed. Our fathers said he wasn't one for rule-breaking. Death, on the other hand, makes more sense."

"The auldjin treats her like his daughter. To him, what's a wee bit of jail time or a lost head," Aronia smiled.

"He might as well. After all, he's lost so much."

Quarz didn't trail off; he just stopped speaking. When Anemone realized he said, "*Our fathers,*" she wondered if Quarz was talking about Spriggan's father or her own. She hadn't heard much about either of them, so his words lingered. Regarding her father, Titania never mentioned him, and neither did Spriggan. Long ago, when she had asked Titania about her father, Anemone was told not to worry about him. Surprisingly, Anemone readily complied, remembering her father had escaped her mind for so long. As old as Spriggan was and looked, he wasn't her father. Even if he had been there for every moment of her life, Anemone wished she knew more about her father.

"Quarz, do you know my father?"

"So, they never told you?" He rubbed his head. "Your dad was a soldier who went missing."

"Missing?"

"Yup. Vanished. Ten years ago. Even if I wanted to tell you more, I couldn't."

Quarz pointed his finger at a sigil on his neck.

"Yer coddin'! I thought the Kingdom banned Ars like that centuries ago. That's the curse of the Marked Tongue."

"They did, but civil loopholes are always a thing."

Anemone shook her head. "Wait, they put the curse on you so you wouldn't talk about my father? Why is he that much of a secret?"

"Not him per se, but what involves him is more—correct." Quarz rubbed his throat.

"Don't worry, Quarz, I won't make you lose your tongue over this."

"Much appreciated, little miss. This merchant needs his voice."

Anemone turned away and tried to hide the shock on her face. The Marked Tongue was a dangerous spell, and anyone placed under it was no minor issue. If the caster or recipient broke the conditions, either could lose their voice. Asking Titania might be out of the question, but she thought Spriggan might tell her. She had heard a few stories of her father here and there, but Spriggan almost avoided talking about him. Titania had wished for anything related to her father to be kept a secret, but Anemone never expected this. Quarz had a look on his face as if he wondered whether it was something he should have told her. As the Dragonkin walked up to Quarz and whispered in his ear, he broke Anemone's focus.

"The Queen has already returned...we don't have the time for this."

After taking a deep breath, Quarz turned away from Anemone and gave her his farewell. Anemone's eyes widened as she looked at her clothes. Anemone waved as she turned to Aronia and told her she would see her tomorrow. When Anemone turned back around, she bumped into someone wearing a hood. They instantly reacted to Anemone, grabbing her shoulders before she flew back. The sight of a Coronaria pin on their cloak caught Anemone's attention, and she looked at their face. Immediately they covered their face and apologized. Aronia grabbed Anemone before leaving. When she pulled out her Grimoire, she cast a spell aloud.

"Grimoire-Ars: Derive: Cake-(Hand)"

The pages of her book flashed open and flipped through themselves. Suddenly c cake appeared in her hand.

"Ye were so ready to rush 'aff I nearly forgot. It's one of yer favs. Mum war cake."

"Nia, I completely forgot."

"Don't wurry. Just make sure you beat yer mum home. Otherwise, I won't hear the end of it from ye."

Anemone had forgotten how much she begged for that cake. After apologizing, she separated from Aronia and began to think about who else would know her father. The thought of learning more about her father excited her mind more and more. She tried to ignore it and promised herself she would ask Spriggan tomorrow.

Once Anemone got to the front of her home, she bribed the Phloem Guards with some of Florentina's war cake. Aronia had her mother's recipe, so well-loved by many as culinary Aurum. Her blended Juglans nuts, spices, seed milk, honey, and cricket flour were an unmatched secret. Anemone didn't know if her mom had arrived back in Tir-noNog, so she wanted to get in and switch out of her torn clothes as soon as possible. With the day so eventful, she forgot about her clothes' condition. She went around to enter through the back of their large tree home. Hopping branch to branch, she did her best not to drop the rest of the cake as she climbed into her room. It was dark enough to get in primarily unnoticed and, thanks to her room, angled in opposition to the moon's light.

"Had an eventful day?" a voice called.

"Mother!?" Anemone yelps, almost slipping. "You're back."

Anemone had forgotten to ask the guards if Titania had already been inside. The bribe was for them to say nothing about her extra training with Spriggan, but now she regretted it. Titania stood with her sword in hand and body erect, staring Anemone dead in her eyes. Anemone saw Titania's long black hair was already untied, which meant Titania's day had finished some time ago. Even so, Titania still wore that crown, and Anemone's eyes focused on it.

"One day, you will wear it and feel the weight of the Thorne Circlet."

"I'm not sure I want to."

Titania was always perceptive, and Anemone couldn't respond to that statement. She was almost hesitant to experience it. Ever since Anemone was born, she could recall Titania leaving in and out of Tir-noNog for all political jabber types. As Anemone aged, the distance between the two naturally grew so giant Anemone had long forgotten her mother's smile. Her mind felt muddled as she continued to stare at the Grimoire. Titania was born into war and lived through it. Unlike her Grandmother Mab and Grandfather Dagda, Titania had survived the war, and their deaths were why she inherited the Thorne Circlet.

The sight of her in an emerald nightgown complimented her torn purple wings and pale skin. Anemone's eyes quickly averted the presence of Titania's torn wings. One rarely caught a glimpse of Titania, not in armor adorned in Lumenopal or wearing some Od-resistant resistant material. Even though she hadn't fought in years, it seemed as if she was still ready to do so at the drop of a leaf. Her lavender eyes darted straight for Anemone's clothes as she straightened her stature.

"You understand that it's not hard to keep track of you as the Queen of these woods."

"Right, the connection to the Lauma tree... eye of the woods and tons of troops." Anemone mocks one of her mother's idioms.

"Although training is essential, I asked you—"

She interrupts, "I know not in *my* dresses. I'm sorry, I'm still training with Spriggan."

"Even if you are more prepared for the exam, he spoils you far too much."

Anemone held up the cake. "The written exam is a cakewalk, don't worry—."

She slammed her scabbard into the ground. "Haughty behavior will get you killed. Is that what *he* teaches you?"

"No. That error in behavior was mine, mother."

"Trials aside, you must be more for more than yourself. The world is changing, and you must strive to be a beacon for your people! We are in a time where Elves, Fae, and Dwarves weren't at each other's throats."

"But Gentiana blasted the kingdom Alberich off the map." Anemone thought to herself.

As Titania continued to explain how pivotal it is that Anemone was born in a lifetime during the Three Crown's Treaty period, she tried to ignore her. Everyone knew three of the strongest Aos-Si kingdoms had united in peace to prevent most large-scale conflict. There were still small-scale battles between smaller groups of Aos-Si throughout Abhainn-Reatha, but few had to kill each other. Only issues between Unseelie, those infected by *Gallu*, and the Seelie, were far more prominent. Many Aos-Si preferred fighting and killing each other for land and resources outside the three thrones. However, Anemone always believed they could work together even if they didn't see eye contact. Even though Titania claimed this was peace, Anemone felt it could be better. She never understood why everyone kept fighting and why Titania had to. A part of her was starting to believe total unity was impossible beyond these walls, but Titania didn't. Anemone would have to carry her mother's beliefs one day and dawn the Thorne Circlet, the Fae Crown. At least, that is what she expected.

"After the Trials, YOU will be posted in Albion," Titania asserted.

Anemone shook her head. "Wait. I thought getting a view of the rest of the world was better for me."

"After my recent discussion with King Gentiana, we'll unite the kingdoms closer through you and his eldest son, Clausa."

"What? Acaulis' brother!?"

Titania nodded, "Your lack of wings makes a grand political statement to create unity, regardless of circumstance. Hopefully, it will also ease his grip on the Lumenopal. Think of it as Dragovian Treaty, but it's between Fae and Elf, instead of Dragons and Avians."

The room swirled around her; even as more words came out of Titania's mouth, the sound disappeared. Only the wind blowing through her room caught her attention. She wanted the wind to carry her away. Of course, she wanted to serve her people, but the world was an open frontier to explore before being sentenced to an uncontrollable fate. Spriggan told stories of Airemul, a Dragovian kingdom that floated in the sky, Tirfo-Thuinn, the civilization under the seas, and the Denizen's lost home, Ganeden. History practically erased them from the world, but their lore kept her going. She hoped to go from Cadet to Comrade-at-Arms and eventually an Anther Trooper in the Arbor Magna to get that opportunity to travel. Although Anemone's duty was to become a pillar for her people, she didn't expect this to be her direction in life. Her future was fleeting.

Titania probably didn't even know how she felt. After all, how could she? Titania was seldom around Anemone and only barked platitudes or rules to follow. Titania walked up to her and held her hands to comfort her. Anemone could feel her body heating up as the urge to flinch at her mother's touch and scream at the top of her lungs nearly escaped her. As she stared into her mother's eyes, there was a glint of concern. It was the same look she had seen on Aronia's face earlier. Never before had Anemone seen such a thing on Titania's face. Every decision made was cold and calculating. Yet, there was something strange about how she gripped Anemone's hand. Her grasp grew weak as if there was a wavering feeling in Titania's heart. When Anemone looked down, she noticed a scar on Titania's hand. Once Titania saw her line of sight, she quickly left Anemone.

Anemone leaned on the wall behind her and slid down. Knowing how Titania was, flailing about wouldn't have achieved much. There was a wall between them, and Anemone didn't know how to get past it. They hadn't talked to each other in a long time, and each conversation lasted for less than a few minutes. Their conversation was one-sided, and she didn't take it as an opportunity for more. Maybe that moment was an opportunity, but now it was gone. They didn't even fight about the dress she had ruined. The urge she had to get closer to her mom was vanishing. Anemone sat on the ground and pulled out the Grimoire.

"At least she didn't see this," she thought. *"I wonder what she was like with grandma and grandpa. I wonder if she felt like I do now."*

As she held her hand over the Grimoire's Arcane Lumenopal, those thoughts almost distracted her from focusing. Although it took a moment, she could connect her Flux to the stone. The immense shine and surge of energy into her body assured her the connection was successful. She opened the Grimoire to place a quill on the first page.

"Grimoire-Ars Inserta: Quill."

The page glowed, and the quill disappeared into the page. Even if what she wanted wasn't going to happen, it didn't change the fact that the trials were still tomorrow. Anemone decided it was good to always put some Ars inside for multi-casting. She cast a few Exalt-Ars Exceed, Xiphos, Scutum, Ward, and Phalanx. They were essential Ars for boosting mobility, offense, and defense. It would be easier to aid her team of five if they were ever in a bind. Anemone grabbed a quiver and bow from her closet. She also reached for the hundreds of arrows she stashed away. Some arrowheads were fractured Vulcan and Sylph Lumenopal, while others were Dwarven Steel. If she couldn't cast any Elemental-Ars, she could at least use the closest thing to it. After loading her quiver and Grimoire with arrows, she added her short sword and shield, knives, a lantern, some rope, and other essentials. Her eyes glanced across her somewhat empty room.

The only things that filled her bookshelf were political dissertations, geographic manuscripts, historical text, and flora guides. As she walked over to it, her hand reached to crack open a hidden compartment on her shelf, and there lay a single book inside that she held dear.

"Memoirs: The Land of Running Rivers," she read aloud.

The book was unregistered and read more like a diary than anything. Anemone's finger ran across the scratched name on the cover. Thanks to the surface condition, she didn't know who the author was. All she could read was "*V—lion Yu—a.*" "V" traveled through unknown lands in a world without the *Gallu*. With their five-band team, they saw the beauties and wonders of their world and faced off against some monster called Mehen.

As she opened the book again, she looked at one of the bestiary pages drawn in it. The creatures had strange names but resembled monsters she had heard. Or from what she could at least gather from the crude art drawn, they seemed similar to the fauna of Abhainn-Reatha. No matter how many times she looked at them, something was off. Anemone gazed at one of them and saw the words *Great Antelope* next to it. What appeared to be horns looked like a dozen crooked arms. Its long face resembled a navigation scope, and what she assumed were its legs were stubby twigs.

"Even though I love this story, I still can't figure these things out."

Every time Anemone turned a page to see another drawing, deciphering what it was, was challenging. She would have never guessed what they were if it weren't for the in-depth descriptions. "V" had even visited a place called Tir-naNog that was almost similar to her home. However, its events didn't match Tir-noNog lore, so she figured it was just a storybook. Besides Spriggan's stories, *this* book excited her to see the world. Sitting in her dark-filled room, she gazed at the starry sky from her window. This time it wasn't enough to give her a small piece of mind, and she couldn't hold back her tears.

Sometimes she thought about what would happen if Tir-noNog disappeared, but she knew it was selfish of her to wish. She wished she could disappear and rid herself of the title of princess, which meant nothing, just like her feelings did to her mother. She saw Rubus walking with other unfamiliar Aos-Si she didn't recognize from her window. As they walked and talked, she wondered if he felt free. Even if he didn't get along with everyone, he could choose how to live his life. To her, that was the true freedom she wanted.

"*I wish things didn't have to be this way,*" she thought as she buried her head into her knees.

WHERE THIS IS

My eyes ached, and my mind flashed blinding light over and over to the point of nausea. When my sight returned, I could see *her* in front of me. Both of us sat as we saw Anemone's memories. My hand clenched the storm swirling in my chest. A cold numbing chill washed over me; her regrets, worry, and awe had become my own. I could no longer separate myself from experiencing her life at that moment. Just like the Tree I had touched before, I was experiencing life. Only this time, it was one person versus many, and it was far more bearable.

Feeling her future ripped from her was more than bitter. Even though she didn't shed a tear, my body did so in her stead. Though I felt terrible for Anemone, it was challenging to say that I genuinely cared. It didn't make sense why she never told Titania how she felt. Even if Titania denied her choice, there was no reason to keep those feelings bottled inside. Oddly, the more Anemone crossed my mind, the deeper I felt the connection between her and myself. I lifted my head for a moment and stared at the Transcendent.

"Why show this to me," I asked her. "Where am I, and what does that have to do with me?"

A tear ran down her face as she sat unfazed. Seeing that tear made me realize she might not be a monster. Perhaps she was just disconnected from her emotions? Moments passed, but she said nothing; it was as if she had never heard me. Before I asked the question again, her eyes eerily slid from the fruit to me.

"I've sat here and observed many lifetimes through these trees, but something drew me to this one. I'd hoped to find myself somewhere in the Memoria that nourished them. Do you recall what Memoria is?"

Hearing the word *Memoria* made my gut flutter, and I could recall the sight of faceless beings telling things, and one of them explained what *Memoria* was. After their words, I heard unfamiliar voices calling out more inaudible words. As they dissipated, the word *Memoria* refocused my mind.

"Memoria is the memory of the soul. It contains every experience of your lifetime. Makes you who you are and is also known as the *Color of the Soul*." My arms folded as I continued.

She nodded in agreeance. "As you die, your soul pours back into the planet, splitting itself into a blank slate of pure Adnero and Memoria as it ascends into the realms beyond."

For some reason, her word made sense to me. I gathered that I was definitely dead from what she said, yet I felt calm. I looked back at my hands and pulled up my sleeve for a bit, and my forearm had already become fully Adnero-like. My eyes looked back at the Adnero-like beings below, and I instinctively understood what they were. The voice from my memory that gave me the answer was condescendingly sweet and snarky, but that sweetness hummed in my ear.

"This isn't the physical world...Those are Hollow-pneuma, aren't they?"

She nodded her head. "Their journeys led to them becoming Memoria-less husks."

I turned back to her. "That still doesn't answer my questions, though. Why—"

Her eye locked onto me and stopped my words, "Those Hollow-pneuma aren't like you...you feel familiar."

"Familiar? How?"

"Even though you are formless to me, I know you." Her voice softened.

"Formless?"

"You look just like them, faceless embers wandering around *Sillih*."

Even though this Tree resembled pure crystal, there was no reflection to see me. Looking at her again, I felt drawn to her, but it wasn't out of familiarity, or at least that's how I felt. When I saw Anemone, I knew she was familiar, but this Transcendent was a complete mystery. Unlike those Hollow-pneuma below, it seemed I was somewhat aware, so maybe my Memoria was still connected to my soul. Even if that was the case, something must have damaged its connection. I knew what Abhainn-Reatha looked like, but my identity was still fuzzy. The only reference I had to myself so far was that Anemone had killed me.

My gut told me it was more than a coincidence that we crossed paths; we had met before. Perhaps there was a connection between the Transcendent and Anemone? Maybe I could learn more about both of them and myself.

"I guess it's the afterlife?"

"This is *Sillih*."

"I don't really see what's silly here." My brows furrowed.

"No, this is the *Sillih Caudex*, you Dolt. The *Tree of Ganeden* in the *Empyrean* Realm."

"Ohhhh, the realm above the Halls of Amenti... Does that mean this Tree is?"

"Precisely, it's what many call the *Etz Hayyim*, the Tree that encompassed all truth.

"So, *this* tree is *that* Tree."

"Yes, it's the *Tree*. Please don't start with me." Her eyes sharpened.

"That means these fruits bear the knowledge beyond good and evil."

"Thank you."

Somehow, that banter also felt familiar, as if it had happened before. Jesting aside, I knew nothing of the *Sillih Caudex*, much less *The Halls of Amenti* or the *Etz Hayyim*. On the other hand, I unconsciously knew that the information would grow more apparent. Memories of my master talking about their search for the *Etz Hayyim, the Tree of Knowledge,* popped up. They needed to know how to stop *something* from happening but never found *The Tree.*

The Halls were said to connect to the Empyrean Realm, where the Celestials roamed, but no one knew how to get there. It was a place between the living world and the metaphysical that became a myth like the Transcendent. In a nutshell, this place was the "Wonderworld" my crazed master wanted to find. My master had dreamed of finding a way there, yet I stood before their very goal. Go figured I'd get here. What a shock that all it took was for you to die to reach it. That being said, something didn't add up.

"If that's the case, why do I see the lives of the living in these fruits? How is that true knowledge?"

She turned away. "The Vitis Fruits contain fragments of the most important events of someone's being. Truth can be relative to the beholder and their experiences."

"Hold on, that sounds a little reducing. All knowledge is just this one being's experiences?"

"Good Glory, you are slow. It's the condensed experience of everything, from the tiniest spec of matter to the most complex being. Seeing only one makes it easier, too—."

"Digest," I interrupted.

The look of scorn she wore almost made me laugh, and I didn't know why. I looked away and focused on the fact that the world's knowledge was in my grasp, yet I didn't feel the awe I thought I should have. Thanks to my missing memories, I don't even know what I had hoped to gain by finding this thing. At this point, the knowledge it offered was looking kind of useless.

"Well, that's cool... can you eat it?"

"You touched the tree and saw what happened, so be my guest."

She gave me a sharp side-eye, so I held my breath as I turned away. Her sass was surprisingly intense. Suddenly I realized all my fear had evaporated, and she was far more normal than I expected.

"Sorry, but my Memoria probably isn't intact. Some of this makes sense, and some is a jumble." I rubbed my neck. "It's hard for me to know what I know."

She stared back at the Vitis and said, "Look, these only allow you to see the Memoria of others connected to you."

"Go figure. Even the Tree of Knowledge limits its knowledge."

The last sentence made me recall my experience from before—me Touching that Tree was mind-numbing. My thoughts clouded my focus so much that I didn't realize her eyes locked on me. She didn't blink for a single moment. It was like a predator, dead set on its prey. Yet her eyes were mesmerizing. The abrupt feeling of my chest compressing broke my focus. I hadn't become a Hollow-pneuma for the time being, but I began to ponder whether I would lose more of myself.

"Umm, Ya need something?"

"You...."

My heart skipped a beat, and I felt my face flush. Not because of how captivated I was but due to not realizing those chains had already bound me in place. As the Trancendant's face got closer, I noticed how the chains sprawled from behind the Transcendent. Soon the chains constricted around my neck, and as I squirmed, the grip of the chains only grew stronger. My neck not snapping instantly was more surprising than the pain itself. Then again, I was a spirit. Before attempting to turn my face, her hands now held it still.

"It's my turn for answers," she murmured.

Although I was a spirit, it felt like her nails pierced into my skull. I could feel the sensation of them burrowing their way inside my head. Little by little, I felt each finger squirm its way deeper inside. No matter how much I struggled, there was nothing I could do. Her hand muffled my screams, and the agonizing experience made my body limp.

Without warning, images flashed through my mind. My arms were bound, and I repeatedly felt pain surging through my body. Once again, I saw an empty-faced Aos-Si, but now they had scarlet hair. After that, a dark dungeon filled the background, and someone else was in front of me.

There was a warm sensation near my abdomen, and I felt something cold pierce inside it. As it glided through, I could feel blood pour from my body, and when I looked down, I felt my eyes strain. The scene of my guts falling out of me flashed in and out of sight. The pain of my bounded wrists and gutted bowls fused with the crushing force of her chains. As she continued to dig, I could see what might have been her memories as well. Stars lit a dark sky, a temple filled with black flames burned a forest, and the word *Volition* flashed. The sight of a large tree burned with that Black Fire and sadness echoed in my heart.

Suddenly Adnero pulsed from my body. Its rhythmic waves flushed through my body and began to surge with every chain link until they reached her. The sound of agony echoed from her as her arm flung itself from my head. The chains suddenly loosened, and I gripped them and continued to surge Adnero. When she flailed her arm in my direction, I jumped back with the chain still in hand. She launched a flurry of chains at me again, and I covered my arms in more Adnero to knock them away. While she lay still distressed, I descended to the ground and made a full-on dash towards the grove of trees.

A sharp constricting pain caught one of my legs running, slamming my face into the ground and pulling my body back towards the Tree without notice. When my eyes could compute what happened, I was strung upside back in its branches by the crystallized fruit. Surprisingly, her face was still calm, as if she wasn't experiencing absolute pain a moment ago.

"Why are you running?" she beckoned calmly.

"Why wouldn't I!? Dead or not, I'm not interested in reliving agony!"

"Reliving agony? What's that?" Her head tilted.

"Agony!!! Y'know!? Pain!"

"I don't understand."

My mind was racing a thousand miles a minute, but she was as confused as I was. The idea that she had been here so long she had forgotten what pain was, eluded me. You would think she still understood if she subjected herself to re-experiencing many lifetimes. Then again, maybe she had experienced so many of them. So many that apathy had overtaken the connection to her feelings. An exasperated huff left my mouth as I saw her tilt her head at me in curiosity.

"Look, that hurt you felt when my Adnero touched you was pain."

"Sorry."

Quickly she dropped me back on the Tree and walked towards the fruit. Her chain reached into the upper branches and grabbed other Viti's fruits to place them next to the one we saw together. I got back up to my feet and rubbed my head. Once again, she signaled for me to return in front of her. Having almost died again, I was more hesitant to avoid dealing with her, but my chances of running away already seemed slim. To add, the world down below was probably just as intimidating. Her eyes locked on me as I stood, trying to weigh my options. Suddenly, I was in front of her again. At this point, it didn't seem like I had much of a choice. Without a beat, she shoved another one into my face.

"I have seen all of these; something about them is familiar, like you. I wish to know who I am," said the Transcendent as she raised another.

The look in her shimmering eyes was somewhat pleading. There was a jarring difference between being nearly murdered and being asked to aid her. Although she didn't outright say she wanted my help, having her continue shoving the damn thing in my face said otherwise. If she said I was familiar, I might see myself in one of these fruits. Either way, it was better than accidentally making her angry in my attempts to say no.

"Fine, I'll help you! Just don't go digging in my head for Memoria, okay."

She nodded, affirming, and I grabbed one of them and peered into the fruit. Oddly enough, it wasn't Anemone's memories I saw, but someone else's.

...The Silver Soldier

Aos-Si bustled through the busy streets of the Four Winds festival, yet it seemed like all the noise of everyone faded to silence. Rubus stood next to Acaulis, turning only his head to look at him dead. The whisper his ears heard in broad daylight had stunned him. Everyone knew Tir-noNog was famous for having ears in every reach of Abhainn-Reatha and Acaulis was bold enough to say it in *their* kingdom. He had heard what he assumed was a ploy by Acaulis' arrogant nature, but he was indeed dead serious. Acaulis always wore an aloof face and had a curve in his voice whenever he spoke. For once, it wasn't there.

"Didn't you hear me, Rubus? I said we could kill the Royals of Albion; we can kill our father. You can get revenge for mother."

Ever since they were young, he swayed his steps and made a scene, but now he was hushed. The Albionian Elven prince was arrogant but not foolish. He never did something or said something he couldn't back up. It was one of the few reasons Rubus respected Acaulis, but this still seemed like a stretch.

"No, I heard you, Acaulis. I was just surprised."

Acaulis leaned over his brother and shrugged his shoulders. "Not excited? You'll get to use that arm of yours again."

"No, it's not that. I just think you're insane." He stopped with a confused nod. "But what's your plan?"

"Patience, dear brother, the time will come for you to know more. Much like the time will come for Tir-noNog to fall. Just know I'll need Daddy's old *Silver Hound* on my side."

Before Acaulis walked off with a wave, he patted Rubus' back. The look of contempt on Acaulis' face made Rubus clench his arm. He felt there was nothing he could say, not even a quip. He recalled that very look the night he had run away. Since escaping that night from Albion, Rubus had never looked back and thought he was free. Now it felt like it was time for him to pay his dues. Rubus reached for Acaulis' arm, and instantly, a brown-haired elf with a star under his eye gripped his arm.

At that moment, he was glad his arm was already numb. Otherwise, he might have felt the full ferocity of their grasp. His eyes were empty when he looked at the elf, and his skin seemed oddly glossy. Its slight polished, crystal-like shine matched his stony vice grip. The Arcane Od pouring from his pores made Rubus quiver. Before he realized it, Acaulis had already disappeared into the crowd, and the other Elf followed without a word. They would be worried if anyone could see and know what he did.

"That *Flux* was unbelievable. I don't believe it. Gentiana completed that damn project?"

Rubus couldn't believe how much Od was flowing from that soldier. Unlike Fae, who could feel Od, Elves could see the Pressure of *Flux*, and Elf's *Flux* was enormous for his age. It was at least double his arm span and was just as strong as a Commander who had fought for decades. This demonstration was a statement from not only Acaulis but Gentiana as well. Rubus understood why Acaulis had them meet away from others. He was foolish to believe he could have gotten away without anyone noticing him missing.

Rubus stumbled to a nearby bench and unbuttoned the rest of his Gambeson uniform as his eyes focused on a single loose cobble in the road. Shoes, hooves, and feet all passed that cobble as it bounced without kicking it up. He stared back at his right arm and clenched it. Rubus had finally gotten free from Albion's clutches, and now it felt like he was back in the hole he belonged.

His thoughts kept racing, and he took a deep breath. Now wasn't the time to panic. After all, he still had a trump card. In any case, even if Acaulis needed him to do anything, he had leverage. He could tell

Commander Airelle what he knew and plea for a trial, or better yet, kill Acaulis, ignore everything, and run again. However, if he did that, he would lose his resources here. He needed the Tir-noNog information loop. Otherwise, he wouldn't find *her*.

"Ye really have a lot on yer mind, don't 'cha?"

He saw that familiar short-cut redhead with a plate of Step Wisent meat and a skewer in hand. When she pointed at his chest, he realized his hand was unconsciously fumbling with the silver necklace he always wore.

"Yer always fiddling with that thing when ye got a lot on yer mind" she continued.

"Yeah, but it's nothing. I can't manage, Aro." He tucked his necklace away.

"Poor Ru has the whole world on his shoulders," she mocked him. "And don't call me Aro. Stick to Aron or Aronia. Otherwise, others will get suspicious."

"Fae culture is weird. You all think nicknames mean Aos-Si are jamming genitals together."

"Haud yer wheesht'. No need to be so crude."

"A modest succubus?" he smiled. "Someone call Stereotype Enforcement."

Aronia rolled her eyes and sat next to him. "What's up? Why'd yoo lose all yer Chione so suddenly?"

"One, I never had any Ice-Ars." He held his breath. "Two."

He paused for a second and the two of them sat in silence. Aronia had known Rubus for a while, and she was the first acquaintance he had made arriving in Tir-noNog. Before he had escaped from one of Albion's research facilities, he met her by chance. They never exchanged words, but something about her made her easy to approach. After seeing her again after he arrived in Tir-noNog, he was surprised she still had a similar vibe.

"Don't worry about it. I'm fine."

She placed her hand on his, "I kno ye think we aren't that close, but I'm here for ye."

He held her hand. "I know. Just know this is something I have to do on my own."

She had a look of disappointment that he was too familiar. Aronia had already told him about his metaphorical wall. She raised her plate of Step Wisent meat, hoping to cheer Rubus up. He could only smile and nod, trying to keep his composure.

"You look like you have something to say."

"And what might that be?"

"You want me to open up and tell you my problem, but I also know something else is on your mind. Is it Wingless?"

Aronia stuffed her face with food and turned away.

"Come on, Aro. That's what? Two years in TirNog and another three in Albion? I think I get some of your nuances."

She kept her back turned before letting out a big sigh of relief.

"Fine, it is! But ye must understand. She's been under a lot of pressure."

"Self-induced, honestly."

Aronia punched him. "I'm serious, Ru, she's been trying to nab her mum's attention for years, and it's finally getting to her."

"Why not tell her to ease off and live her own life? Titania doesn't need her around."

"That's the problem, Ru. Nin wants to be needed, and it's hard."

"For you or her?"

"Could ye just let me vent and not have me evaluate my feelings for, I dunno, five minutes?"

"Mmm... I'll give you five, four, three, two—."

It took Aronia a second to realize he was messing with her. Rubus knew how much Anemone meant to Aronia, so he was willing to listen even if he didn't want to. Her comment of the world on his shoulders wasn't too far-fetched, and he was starting to feel it. Rubus wasn't close to anyone, and after everything he had been through, he wished he had an ear to listen. He knew she would be in danger if she learned anything as much as he wanted to. Instead, he chose only to listen. As he heard more about Anemone, he started to see she, too, was born into a world that didn't need her.

"She does the same thing too."

"What do you mean?"

"You also hold on to your left arm when something bothers you. Seriously Ru, what's wrong?"

He didn't even realize he was holding his arm, and after learning more about Anemone, Rubus almost empathized with her. A part of him felt a bit jealous. At this point, he was beginning to wonder how soft he had become after coming to Tir-noNog. Rubus shook his head at his feelings as he looked into the sky. Beforehand, he always had a reason to stay alert. Perhaps this time, he could be vulnerable. Maybe it was time to let go; Aronia was strong enough to support him. Now he wouldn't have to be afraid of Acaulis.

"Aro, it's about Acaulis."

Words abruptly stopped coming from his mouth as something in the distance caught his eye. The design was unremarkable; a simple white canvas mask covered the face. What stuck out was the lack of eye holes and the gray fog-shaped blotch on it. Its design felt eerie in a sea of facemasks representing a season and elemental Od. Suddenly like trumpets sounding, it hit him. Rubus saw that mask. It was the mask he saw before someone killed his mother before his eyes. It was also there before *she* went missing and the night he was allowed to flee Albion. Even if he had only seen it three times, how could he have forgotten that design? It made his blood boil as his face flushed with heat. He rushed off, leaving Aronia behind, and didn't look back.

Rubus scurried with his frantic breath, his eyes erratically darting left and right to find the mask he had now lost among the crowd. It had been so long since he had last seen it that his mind had almost forgotten it. He would have noticed sooner if it weren't for the masked-filled festival. Weaving in-between crowds, he kept chasing that mask seeing it in the corner of his eye at almost every turn. It was starting to feel like he was in a sea of covered faces. Every face with a masked looked like it.

Left and right, his head swiveled as music and voices calling about made him nearly lose his footing. He was starting to feel like he had been running around for hours. When he turned, he saw it finally staring at him from across a group of Elves pushing each other around. The fog-masked stranger stood still as if they knew Rubus had found them. As Rubus took another step, they walked back into the crowd with a wave.

"Lycan-shit! They know!"

He bolted straight ahead, pushing everyone out of his way. As he got to the crowd's edge, Rubus's leg crossed one of the Elves that moved another. As he stumbled, a boot crossed his face and stunned him. Although he was angry, his focus on something far more critical kept him moving, or at least until he heard the *D*-word.

"Watch it you dammed Dökkálfar."

It was the name of an elf with the darkened sclera or who had contact with the *Gallu*. Few ever spoke of them as they were considered evil by Elven standards. His feet stopped moving, and he couldn't decide which way to go. Rubus could have easily ignored what was happening, but instinctively he couldn't let it go. No context was needed, as Rubus knew that respect was out of the window when an Elf yelled that word. When someone uttered that word to your face, its weight resounded as a response. Rubus' response was uncuncion and it was too late; his body already moved. Before her healized it, Rubus planted his boots in the back of the Elf that screamed that word.

He felt a tug from the back of his head, and he already knew they had a hold of the band across his eyes. Falling into a handspring, he raised his other leg and tried to land his other boot on another elf's face, but they were quick. He stood up and wanted to rush him, and his arms got locked into a headlock. When he turned to see who grabbed him, a blow slugged him in his side. The shock of the collision forced a gasp out of him, and he could see his vision blur for a second. His mind blanked for a few moments, but he could feel the back of his head and his fist aching from an impact as he heard someone yell.

"By order of the Lauma Family Monarchy, I Ninlil Anemone order this senselessness to CEASE!"

...Albion Trio

Rubus gazed into the sky as he wiped the blood from his face. It was hard for him to hold back as he heard the mob hollering, ringing in his ear. Once again, his instincts had overwritten his judgment. The suckered punch he had just received made him lose the sensation in his face. Much to his surprise, Anemone had stood up and offered aid. She always seemed irritated by him, and he could never understand why. Everyone else usually fought him for being a Dökkálfar, but she seemed to have different reasons. Even if Aronia told him she had a sense of justice, helping him did seem like the right thing to do.

Fae usually had a more *don't look or touch policy* regarding conflict. Elves, on the other hand, were culturally different. If it weren't for Tir-noNog's policy on open discrimination, the situation might have been more akin to what he was used to, a constant Dominance hierarchy. A Blackened Sclera cadet slowly rose from the crowd and extended their hand with Rubus's jacket.

"I appreciate that you stepped in. I'm sorry I left you to fight them alone. Those Ljósálfar stole my veil, and I tried to get it back. I kinda froze."

Rubus hadn't realized that someone else was involved in that skirmish, much less his uniform flying off. To think another Dökkálfar was in distress, he felt a little better for intervening. Sadly, he had lost his target and could not find them without a trace. He dusted himself off and spoke to the other Dökkálfar without looking at him.

"Don't worry about it being three-on-one. I don't blame you for running. Besides, I have a knack for trouble either way."

Rubus was shocked to see another fist hadn't flown into his face. As he grabbed his Gambeson, he saw a familiar black tattoo under amber-colored eyes when he looked around. That tied-back messy green hair he tried combing out so many times matched the face of an Elf he thought he'd never see again. Their voice smiled at him as they appeared from the crowd with a wink.

"You really have to learn to punch with your fist and not your face."

"Shut it, Rowan," he smirked. "I don't want to hear that from someone who's never thrown a punch."

"Gasp! Your words! They cut! Oh, so deep, so very deep," Rowan flamboyantly gestured. "I'm but a fragile mage. My hands are far too delicate for your type of roughness."

Rubus raised his arm, and they bumped elbows. Rowan put him in a headlock and ruffled his hair as they laughed.

"You should be dead. How are you even here? Then again, you've always been crafty.

"Crafty sounds so crude. I prefer slick and smooth far better. Also, who's the kid?"

"A Rando, don't worry about him. I'll assume Timber is here too?"

"You don't see that Minotaur of a Dwarf choking the Lycan-shit out of those Elves?"

Rowan pointed to his right, and Rubus turned to his side. He folded his arms and shook his head as he saw the towering Aos-Si strutting towards them. His arms stretched wide with an elf in both hands suspended like a bag of Russets. Rubus was amazed to see his former companions were still alive. From that two-second interaction, he knew nothing had changed about them. Rowan still curved his voice and moved his hands to every word. In comparison, Timber was still a moving mountain that would give even a Minotaur trouble in hand-to-hand combat. The only difference was his haircut changed from a low cut to a curled mid-fade Mohawk.

"Are you seriously doing farmer walks with their bodies?" Rubus punched Timber in the chest.

"Yeah, you might snap their necks." Rowan laughed.

"Oh. Sorry about that."

The moment he dropped their unconscious mouth-foaming bodies, Rubus noticed the sound of the crowd shifting. They no longer had the energy to excite a fight. He quickly grabbed Timber and Rowan as they rushed through the busy streets of the festival. In the distance, he could see a Sargent Major forcing their way through the mob.

After a few minutes of running around, he felt confident they were in the clear. He spent most of his time blending in the background for over two years, and the last thing he wanted was to get caught. When he turned around to check back on the two, they both had hand-skewer finger foods. As usual, they ran at the same clock as each other. Rubus stared at their full plates and pinched the bridge of his brows.

"How did you have the time?"

"You were too focused on losin' the Armada to notice us sneaking food," Rowan snickered.

Rubus facepalmed. "Look, I'm trying not to get any special attention here. Airelle already made me his favorite Lap runner, so the last thing I need is your absurdity and his stature getting me more Arbor Magna attention. Also, why are you here?"

"We could ask the same thing," Timber spoke. "Didn't Gentiana announce you as dead?"

"I would know that; how?"

"Well, there was this whole PSA on the *mysterious* research explosion we caused. We figured you'd know about your handiwork. Just be grateful we scoured the lands for you." Rowan snapped his finger with a point.

Timber shoved his oversized hands across Rowan's face.

"It's LS. We were dragged into Albion's Joint Soldiers Coalition by Gentiana's lotto.

"Speak for yourself. I knew the Elvy had more lives than a Were-felid." Rowan pushed his hand away. "Besides, Acaulis is an asshole who hates Gentiana more than Ru does. As he says, "One Elf's trash is another one's treasure."

"Figure's Acaulis would feel that way, but what about that lottery you mentioned?"

"Yeah. Apparently, it was a random drawing of soldiers who'd join this year's Intra-kingdom Accolade trials."

"And Acaulis personally delivered our tickets."

Rubus fiddled with his necklace. As *delighted* as seeing them alive was, he knew how unfortunate it was for them to be here. It also proved his theory that Acaulis was more than trouble. That explosion from that night inside one of Albion's Research and Development facilities should have been their last, and when they had gone their separate ways, Rubus assumed they had perished. The secrets they had learned from that night were far too valuable.

"Do any of you know some of the other soldiers chosen?"

"Only one, and it was Willow," Timber said.

"Wait, but Willow was another experimental Silver Soldier. I thought the "SS" serum killed her."

"Nope. The bitch lived and got a huge temper problem afterward. Also, I think I remember seeing Birch somewhere around here."

Seeing Acaulis might have been a stretch, but two other Elves who received the "SS" Serum couldn't have been coincidental. Rubus remembered both names when he was in Albion's research facility. The only thing he didn't understand was why Acaulis wanted to involve them. There was nothing to gain from having these two participate in whatever scheme he had, much less himself. If anything, Rubus would do his best to ruin Acaulis' plans. Either way, he knew Tir-noNog was going to become a battlefield. Now he only had to figure out when and why?

"That confirms my hunch. The invasion of Tir-noNog has finally begun."

Timber cut in. "You're missing the part where no one told us to do the *invading* Rubus.

"I know you trust him, Timber." Rubus raised his right arm. "But he's not the king you think he is."

"No, Rubus, it isn't about trust. War doesn't seem beneficial. Aos-Si populations are shrinking, especially those who can wield Ars. Not to mention Lumenopal is beginning to run low. Why would anyone want war?"

"I'm disappointed, Timber. You seem to forget Resource Wars are always an option."

"Of course! Scarcity drives up prices. How could I have done such a thing?"

"Who cares about that?! Just tell me what's the plan." Rowan threw his arms up.

Rubus sat in silence before he spoke. At first, he had thought he could avoid anything with Albion until he found *her*. His trail had run cold now, but if he had helped Acaulis, he might get more information on the Silver Soldier Project and what they did with *her*. As he stared at his right arm, Rubus knew the price might be steep, even if it meant double-crossing Gentiana.

"I don't trust Acaulis, but we'll play along for now. We'll take him down a peg if he's up to no good. It's about high time these upper-class zealots lose their top spot."

"I guess the *Boys* are back!" Rowan raised his elbow.

Timber and Rubus looked at each other and bumped their elbows with Rowan. Once again, the masked stranger appeared in his line of sight, tempting him. This time he was next to another masked stranger with long black hair. But before he made his move, Spriggan stood in front of him.

"I need a moment of your time, Lads."

MEMORIA AND CONNECTIONS

I was viewing the events of that night from both of their perspectives. As I stopped looking at the fruit, I remembered more about what I had seen. To be exact, I knew the name of the Aos-Si he was looking for. I knew it because it was an uncommon name for an Aos-Si, Chimera. All Aos-Si shared that they were named after plants somehow, be it their shape or form, yet Chimera was different. I didn't know why I knew that, but something inside me told me that was the answer. Maybe there was a chance I was Rubus, and this was my life before I met my master, or perhaps she was my master.

After that realization, sights of vast mountains with endless green and red forests and expansive prairies with seas of flowers appeared in my mind. It seemed I had roamed the land, but something in my heart told me it was aimless. Suddenly my heart and head grew fuzzy as the sight of dark red hair flowing in the wind contrasted with an azure sky had overwritten my thoughts. My throat grew dry, and my mind went blank. Every scene of me roaming wonderous lands filled my mind with a blank face with scarlet hair.

A sense of desire fluttered as if I was looking for something to grasp but never found it. More unfamiliar faces appeared, but they all seemed expected and had dozens of expressions. Some were smiles; others were vicious scowls, terror-filled gasps, or tear-filled eyes. I didn't know them yet, but it felt like I did. None of them made me think about the ambivalence as the faceless redhead did. Jubilance brightened my heart, and at the same time, it sank with a bitter weight of sadness. With my mind bogged, I decided to stand and pace around.

"I wonder who that was?" I mumbled.

"Who?" The Transcendent asked.

"I don't know, but they had deep red hair."

A glint appeared in her eyes. "What did you see?"

My spine shivered like it did the first time we made eye contact. A pain in my chest swelled, and I could feel a cold sweat pour over me. Something about that glint made me uneasy, and there was something important about her that they needed to know.

"You're beginning to remember something, aren't you?" She beckoned my attention.

That question seemed challenging to answer. Without my full memories, I didn't have a clear answer. And thanks to the Transcendent scaring me shit-less, I didn't want to. However, the more I focused, the more I remembered that mask Rubus had seen. I was also looking for someone and noticed that mask during that search. My mind ached, and a conversation between Acaulis and me arose. He warned me about someone powerful, someone I had a connection with. After that, my memories jumped around to an explosion where I suddenly found myself immobilized. There was a lab experimenting on something and someone. I also learned Gentiana poured most of his resources into the Silver Soldier Project to create the "SS" tonic. Only his closest officials knew because no one wanted the other kingdoms to realize they had gotten their hands on an Eidolon.

"What's an Eidolon?"

She had cracked her first smile, and it was from ear to ear. Even the skin around her eyes folded as they locked on me.

"Eidolons are beings chosen as vessels for Celestials or other powerful beings. Their connection to Od far exceeded Aos-Si, Therianthrope, Dragon, or Gallu."

Instantly, a sharp pain entered my head again, and my hands clenched as the memories connected to it faded. I looked at the Transcendent to make sure they weren't digging into my head again, but it wasn't the case. There was an unbelievably drilling sensation pulsing through my head. Abruptly the image of a red-haired Aos-Si flew into my mind again. She was still faceless, but just the thought of her made my knees weaken and drop me to my knees. I could feel my senses unconsciously trying to burn her away, and I didn't know why. The more I tried to focus, the throbbing intensified. Quickly I turned to the Transcendent again, hoping to distract myself.

"How does seeing these things help you?"

"These fruits only show memories of what is relevant to the one who holds it. As long as I peer into them, I cannot see what you see, no matter what."

"That's strange. Is it because we don't share Memoria?"

"Precisely. Memoria is erratic and strange. The chain of memories links every moment that connects to your very being."

"And you'll learn more about yourself by finding out about me?"

"I'm hoping so. Little by little, the Memoria will recreate the links in your memories; hopefully, they connect to mine."

"This is a friggin drag," I sighed.

Those words resonated with me as if I constantly said everything was a drag; after admitting that, another scene played in my head. This time, I saw Rubus across from me. He lay sprawled on the floor with a large bruise on his face. I noticed his lips moving, so I knew he was speaking to me, but it wasn't clear.

She raised Anemone's Memoria back into my face, and I stuck my hands out to grab it but paused. Two of her other chains held more Fruits, and I felt a powerful unconscious hesitation. Without much choice, I looked into the other two; one involved Spriggan, and the other was Titania.

...Passing by

The scene was a blood bath. Arbor Magna troop's bodies lay stretched across the forest floor. Some with torn limbs, others with holes punched through their bodies, yet only one Minotaur lay dead. A sonic boom erupted as an ax cut through the wind. The bleeding eyes of another Minotaur damaged from battle darted left to right as it followed swift but silent steps through the upper canopy. The other Minotaurs were all watching for the shadows of nightfall closing in on them as they huffed for air. Each of them stood covering their allies' peripherals. They knew it would be hard to keep up with whatever was hunting them with light fading.

The Minotaur with Cinnabar Lumenopal stepped forward and breathed flames from its nostrils. After a roar, a blast of fire seared the tree leaves above, scorching the air. A cry of agony echoed above as a body fell from the tree and rolled on the floor. It beat its chest in victory, but it was a victory too early celebrated. A pillar of earth lunged itself into its abdomen and caused it to keel over. Its comrades turned to it, and Spriggan fell from above, forcing his spear-like scepter into its spine. His strike was so quick and so precise the Minotaur died instantly.

Before another Minotaur brought its pillar-sized ax down to split Spriggan in two, a spire of earth impaled its arms. Its arm took the impact rather well and only delayed the blade's drop. The slowness created more than enough time for Spriggan to fade into the dark bushes of the woods. In peak rage, it ripped the ax from the cracked earth and tossed the weapon into the distance. The ax spiraled through the air shredding everything in its path, including another tree, right before it lay between the eyes of another Arbor Magna solder. As it sniffed about, it found where Spriggan was hiding and ran toward him. Before he could get close enough, a sudden gust of wind howled and blinded all but that Minotaur. With sheer instinct, he reached for Spriggan, but when his hand closed shut, he realized Spriggan was already gone.

"Pu ni eht eert!" It roared.

The Topaz Minotaur launched into the air, instantly catching up to Spriggan with surprise. He swung his boulder-like arm, and Spriggan raised his staff to block it. The blow was too powerful and sent him flying into the sky. Blades of water flew from the canopy, sliding into the deep wounds that already coved its body. In a moment, it was diced in midair, spilling its blood and guts on everything below. Another Minotaur snapped and roared in rage. Not only at their fallen allies but at the pain of them set ablaze.

The rest of the Arbor Magna soldiers moved in and launched explosive Vulcanus-Ars at the blood-soaked Minotaurs. They all ran towards the group of soldiers, but a giant wall of earth rose between them. The Minotaurs repeatedly beat the wall of craggy rock until slowly, the only sound left in the woods was the crackling of fire sizzling on their robust flesh. Commander Airelle appeared from the darkness and called into the night sky.

"Come back down here, you old fool!"

"Hohoho," Spriggan chuckled. "How did you know I wasn't dead? These old bones are pretty weary, Rellzy."

"You're 250 cycles past expiring. If *death* wanted you, she would have already done me a favor," Airelle snickered. "And quit calling me that! Not even my spouse does it!"

Spriggan sniffed about as he descended.

"Minotaur blood is so meaty and fat. I hear it makes a lovely roast."

"I'm more of a heifer lover myself."

"How do you stomach them, Commander Airelle?" A younger soldier squirmed.

As he wiped seared blood off his face, he yelled at the soldier.

"It's called *Culture* Green-wing! And don't worry about dead bodies. Hurry and secure the caged Aos-Si."

"Relax, Airelle. They live in a different time."

"Your showboating is no help, Sprigs! What is the Academy doing!? Seven of these slackers got slaughtered. For three/fourths of a squad to be taken down so easily—"

His fingers clenched his forehead as his words halted. The two sat on a log and observed the rest of the soldiers tending to the caged Aos-Si. Arielle pulled out a pipe and some dry leaves. He spat at the floor with his brows furrowed, and a genuine look of disgust grew. Spriggan tapped Airelle on his back, but he understood his frustrations. They both agreed the soldiers were too young and inexperienced for such a job.

"The council of Nine shafted them! They knew they weren't ready. Those old maggots have no sense."

"Agreed, but what can we say? The council wants to keep the stronger ones on reserve."

"For what! If those idiots just gave us two more Sargent ranks, we would not have had this many casualties!"

"I beg to differ. We had some rough times ourselves. Just think about the Dragons we've hunted."

When they were young, the Arbor Magna was far more ruthless. They would throw only two of you in a ring with a Minotaur. Sure, they might have had their eyes gouged or an arm missing, but one could quickly kill four Green wings without much effort if they weren't focused. Most of the Phloem guards present had not seen legitimate conflict in years. They were all too comfy behind the safety of Tir-noNog's barrier and easily underestimated the threats outside it, in Airelle's eyes, leaving most of the stragglers to defend their home.

It didn't help that most veterans from their old days were dead. Although the few left stuck in classrooms to future prep soldiers,

Airelle felt their workforce was cut and coddled. Field experience was the most crucial factor in their development, and many of the knights had only slain a few giant bugs. Recruits were disadvantaged, with few leaders who had faced more than Insecta in the field. Both were Provosts who had retired and joined the Academy to train up-and-coming Tir-noNog troops. They had seen the worst of wars and wanted nothing more than to ensure they prepared the next generation. Sadly, for the fresh recruits, the forest was getting more dangerous. It was so bad that even field experience was getting them killed.

"Most of our damn Fae are Sh'fae, or Neu'fae were at a serious disadvantage."

"Careful now. Those are trying words."

"You know I do not mean that, Sprigs! I don't look down on anyone who wants to get in the dirt, but *this* hurts. A battlefield is a place for H'fae to die and the occasional bold one. It's not supposed to be like this."

"You're glad Daisy stayed as an inner wall Apothecary, aren't you?"

He huffed his chest. "You're damn straight! But if I ever told her that, she'd compare herself to—" he trailed off.

"Tomwood. I know his Falliversary just passed, like many of our sons." He placed his hand on his shoulder.

"Seven dead, and the rest are injured for malnourished Nomads, Elves, and a few straggling Dwarves. And the male didn't even make it."

How Spriggan heard the last sentence made him already know what would be said next.

"We don't have enough males to fight, raise kin, or build! You can't tell me you don't see this pattern?"

"You're seriously stuck on this depopulation thing, aren't you?"

"Not just that! The rising KleptOdmania creates Od-less, the increased foreign Aos-Si, Gentiana's expanding control on Lumenopal and medicine? Come on, Spriggs, that war was planned! Lost war, my ass, that war was a loss."

Spriggan knew the toll of the Lost war. It killed most of the males in Tir-noNog, leaving mainly women to raise the young. It had become one of the main contentions of the Cabinet of Nine to increase the immigration of H'fae from other tribes and kingdoms. Thanks to most Fae traditionally being nomadic, it originally wasn't hard. Traveling throughout Abhainn-Reatha, many nomads would wander through and aid in the birth of kin, but the land's danger kept them scarce. Arielle believed this was a part of Gentiana's scheme, but Spriggan did not mind him. His conspiracy of Tir-noNog forced to accept non-Fae foreigners into Tir-noNog was outlandish.

"We are all united under Tir-noNog's banner, did you forget?"

"We are. But *them*?" Airelle pointed to the caged Aos-Si. "They only get a place of refuge. You know Aos-Si don't blend well. Muspell! We Southern Fae can hardly deal with the frigid Northerners. Remember what the Snow Fae did to us?"

Spriggan did, but it was beside the point. With most males being from other Aos-Si or Fae cultures, they raised the children with different beliefs than Tir-noNog. He believed that a solidified identity or a vital cause kept kingdoms around. If there were too many different views, infighting was bound to happen. He was not against mixing cultures, but he understood they needed a consistent identity for a strong kingdom, making them stand as one.

"I'm telling you, Sprigs, if all we have are Sh'fae and Pupas, Tir-noNog will fall. Gentiana's been planning this since the beginning!"

"Oh, hush Rellzy. Calling the remaining H'fae Pupas won't help. They're just inexperienced."

"No, you listen. Strong H'fae are the foundation, and strong Sh'fae are the support columns of kingdoms. Neu'fae are the windows! If there is no strong foundation, you can't build a stable home."

"Good Glory. Did you call your daughter a window?"

"Is that all you got from that?"

"Then let me ask you. What do you prefer? Only our sons are dying, or all children."

Arielle shook his head. "Don't ask me that. Because you already know the answer."

"What, Rellzy? What do I know?"

"War never stops, and someone or something must die for someone or something to live."

Arielle opened his Grimoire, and a small mortar and pestle popped out. He added individual strains of dried leaves and buds, grinding each one briefly before adding the next. His movements were slow and smooth, wasting little effort with each grind. His eyes stared only at the pestle the whole time. Even as a leaf fell near it, he didn't move. Instead, he used the force of his swaying hand to blow it out of the way. His pipe stayed still on his lips as he completed his grinding process.

As he lit it with a Tyndre spell, Spriggan pulled out a flask. For a few moments, they didn't speak a single word. In the distance, they watched the other soldiers tend to the trapped Aos-Si. All of them had their bodies washed with Undine-Ars and soap the soldiers carried. Spriggan handed him his flask, and Airelle gave him his pipe. The both of them indulge in each other's vices savoring the taste. Airelle swallowed the fermented brew, and Spriggan held his breath. At the same time, they both let out a breath as they switched back to their own.

"Which do you think they would have preferred? Smokes or Brews?"

"Fokker never liked my brews, even as a Green-wing. I doubt he'd choose it."

"But Titania turned him into a drinker. Not to mention he loves sweets and spices. That blend is for him, without a doubt. He had taste just like Lydia and Tomwood."

Spriggan took a slow swig and wiped his mouth before he spoke. "Thank you for that...I appreciate it."

"He was my student, a true soldier. I knew him just like my sapling." Airelle nodded. "But I have to say I don't think any of them would agree with your plan."

"I know," Spriggan agreed. "But Lydia, Fokker, and Tomwood died for our home, and we might as well make the best of their sacrifice. The time has come for Titania's return, and soon, everything will begin."

"We're finally going to kill that bastard... I thought I'd die before seeing Gentiana's blood spill upon one of our blades."

Spriggan took another swig before he put his drink away. He got up and checked on the status of the Aos-Si clean-up. As he gazed upon them, less than a third had the will to be grateful. Most of the Aos-Si were so traumatized that emptiness now caged their spirits. Spriggan knew all Therianthropes weren't cruel but telling that to any of them wouldn't mean much. His mind wandered to the group of refugees outside of Tirno-Nog's walls.

"Do you think the Coldwater District is safe for them? Even without us patrolling that area?"

"None of the captured Aos-Si seems to have a *Flux* strong enough for Od, meaning they were probably breeding stock. Coldwater is much safer for them."

"You and I know there's bad blood between Demies and Aos-Si, though."

"Then why ask? You already know that's something none of us want to think about, Spriggs. The Council of Nine only gave them the rights to lands for that awful Safety Net plan."

"I was honestly thinking aloud," Spriggan scoffed. "I often forget how cruel self-preservation can be."

"You need to stop thinking about it. The Amnesty allowed that area to become as lawless as the Wildlands, not us."

"If only I could turn a blind eye like you. Cruelty is one of those things I can't let go of."

"It's survival, not cruelty, Spriggs. Even if Demies are half-beast, we all have an animal in us. Many pretend they don't."

Airelle's voice was hollow, but Spriggan could only nod as he pictured days from his youth when he roamed the lands. He hoped there was a silver lining with them being allowed foot in Tirno-Nog, but that was not the case. Most Demi's had no home, were torn between two worlds, and were enslaved to most of their Therianthrope kin. It didn't help their Aos-Si kin also ostracized them because of their appearance.

A deep sigh left his old dry lips as he couldn't help but think of Fokker again. It was the eighteenth anniversary of his death, and he had planned to pour his brew over his grave, but life had been busy for him. Spriggan was helping Anemone with her training, patrols with The Phloem Guard, and preparing the coups d'état against Gentiana influences. After a few more steps, he realized the extremeness of his earlier stunt; being old was the worst part. Not being able to move as well as he did in his youth made him rethink his trip to the grave tonight. The guilt of forsaking the death of his son was stronger. After all, today's brew has aged for five years, and even Airelle was impressed.

Spriggan turned to Airelle and signaled for him to gather everyone up and head back without him. Arielle knew Spriggan had planned to do it before the sun completely set, but they had missed their mark with the hunt. The two shook hands and pressed foreheads before they went their separate ways. It didn't take Spriggan too long to reach the depth of the woods to find the tree where he had planted the purple flowers. The season for their bloom had already passed, yet they stayed forever in color for some reason. Fokker was a miracle man with plants and brought even the most withered plants back to life. Fokker convinced him to get into brewing and medicinal herb blending. He took out a second bottle and poured it near the tree's trunk with a light prayer to the spirit of Lauma.

A sudden chill rolled down his spine, turning his head to see a looming figure in a black robe. The world around him abruptly lost its color. Every hue, including the dusk-colored sky, was mute to monochrome.

"So, the time has come for your return." He kneeled with his back turned.

"Oh, come now... it's only been a little over a century. How about a smile, you geezer."

"Don't patronize me, false Celestial!"

"Wow, no need for that rage. Save it for later. When we meet again, cycle 1035."

The voice was initially far away, but their covered face was suddenly earshot. Spriggan hurled a tempest in their direction without turning around. Dust clouds erupted as blades of wind cleanly sliced nearby branches to bits. As the smoke cleared, only a tree-deep crater remained without the stranger. Spriggan placed his hand over his eye patch and clenched his face. His eye scanned the environment, and the world regained its color in a flash.

"Their timing couldn't have been worse. I hope *she's* ready."

...Mothers and desires

Titania sat on the windowsill of her room, gazing at the setting sun as her mind stayed fixed on the streets below. She firmly placed one of her hands on the hilt of her sword while the other held a bottle. Many of the youths frolicked through the main road eyeing everything in sight. The presence of a Priestess and Phloem Guards ahead halted their merry dances and smiles. Running towards the children was an Aos-Si with lifeless eyes who threw a tantrum as they shrank and expanded. They passed dozens of other Aos-Si, only knocking over two others. Like clockwork, more Priestesses and Phloem Guards showed up to subdue the rabid Aos-Si and the other two he touched. Soon after, the crowd in the background whispered amongst themselves. Seeing the panicking of the groups below, Titania could already imagine what the Aos-Si murmured as they shook their heads. She knew those symptoms of *that disease* made her shudder.

Titania had expected today that the Celestials would allow a celebration without worry. After taking one more sip from her bottle and realized it was empty, much like her expectations. She reached for another bottle of aged Piorra-Fiann Mead and dropped the one she had on a table knocking over two more empty bottles. As her eyes looked at the bottle in her hand, she focused on the three fading sigils and markings on her arm. Soon a familiar scent of dried cherries and apples filled the air as she drank her mead.

"The cases of *KleptOdmania* are getting worst, Titania."

"Florentina, you old witch—you show yourself!" Titania groaned.

"Unruly as always. Truly Dagda's blood is strong with you."

"So, what do you expect me to do about the Od-Sappers?"

"Od-Sappers? If only poor Anemone would hear you." Florentina shook her head.

"As you are now, nice and toasted? Nothing. But when you stop drinking, your problems away—"

"Hush! I already know the bloody Council of Nine is overstepping their boundaries."

Titania rolled her eyes at Florentina. She knew how contagious *KleptOdmania* was and how it was common enough to notice in a crowd. However, Titania knew something was amiss. Occasionally, a single touch from someone with *that disease* could instantly drain some of your Od, but it did not spread that fast. Even in her moment of bliss, she couldn't ignore the increasing incidents. Two had occurred in a week when she was last here and three more in her absence. It was almost a minimum of five per month, nearly double last year. She had heard from Spriggan that the Council was abducting anyone who demonstrated unruly behavior. It was as easy as a finger-point to round someone up. If that person was an Od-less, it made the task even more accessible. Just thinking of the Od-less made her wonder how Anemone was.

Titania turned back to Florentina and asked her for the status of the locations in the Accolade Trial. She wanted to ensure the areas had no threat above Level Four near the testing sites. Florentina explained much of the Doggerland was clear of any *Gallu*-Utukku that would be too much for cadets to handle. With this year's recruits being less skilled than the last.

"What's the rate of Od-less predicted?"

"Even more will become Od-less. Thanks to the analysis level of the Pylons, they believe there will be more cases of KleptOdmania, especially Sylph users."

"First, the terrible tremors due to the lack of Oread, then the lack of Vulcan and Undine began causing widespread droughts. Now Sylph is fading. What will become of our world without Od?"

"The Arbor Magna research team estimated that the land will become barren in less than a score."

"I guess even less Aos-Si would be with Sylph Od.

They had found a correlation between those born with the Od and the depth of a Pylon's wells. Most near Tir-noNog ran at least fifty feet deep and emitted a natural flow of Sylph Od. Almost a century ago, you could taste the bitter flavor Sylph Od left in the air, but now it was dry. With every generation producing about a hundred offspring, that sensation decreased tremendously. Thanks to the research team's efforts, they learned the age of Sylph was no more.

Outside of Tir-noNog, Abhainn-Reatha was slowly dying, and Titania could feel it through the Lauma tree. After Oread Od dwindled, land bounties became less plentiful. Once the Undine decreased, rains lessened, and as Vulcan followed, the winters got shorter and summers dryer. Now it was the Sylph turn, and now Od-less was rising. Everything was a slow burn passed from one era to another, but Tir-noNog and Albion somehow prospered.

As Titania sipped from her mug, she realized that it had been almost a month since she returned home. It was nearing the dead of night, and she had yet to see Anemone. Anemone had been training under Spriggan for a few years, and Titania wanted to test her skills before leaving for her next expedition. Most of their conversation, from her perspective, flowed rather well. Titania told Anemone what was best, and she followed. Only recently, she began to doubt herself when she spoke to Anemone. A part of her was afraid to talk to her since the last time they conversed; it ended on bad terms. Titania knew Anemone was proud of her for fending off threats and securing more Lumenopal for their home, but lately, there was a hint of displeasure in Anemone's smiles. Titania looked at the sigil on her arm again and shook her head.

"I know I've put it off long enough now that the Council is scrambling for answers. We don't have much time. The barrier is failing."

"That seal Vermillion made is almost broken, Titania. It won't be much longer before he is free."

"Hopefully, I'll be dead by then. Before that happens, I'll send Anemone to Albion."

Florentina's jaw dropped. "Spriggan is an old Tengu! His visions are foolishness! Are you going to listen to him!? Are you not tired of breaking that child's heart?!"

"Heartbreak is good for her... It'll keep her realistic. You and Hibernica need to worry about those other fools."

"Hmph, if it's something you cannot stab, all you do is run from it!"

Titania paid no attention to Florentina's remarks. She was on her third pitcher, and her drink was starting to ease the pain in her feet. The flavor of sweet, spiced pears and cherries always made her feel warm. The taste made Florentina's continued yapping in her ear about her slacker nature bearable. Even though Titania was Queen, she left much of her public image to Florentina and her attendant Hibernica in her stead. The two had seats in the Cabinet of Nine, and an elder Fae, her father King Dagda, was appointed. Hibernica and Florentina had known her long enough to speak on her behalf.

Titania's mind wandered to her days in the Wildlands. The feeling of the scorching desert and glass-like grains of sand on her skin made her blood pump. Like the dry conversations of politics, she wanted to be away from these walls. She was glad The Council handled everything. After Dagda had passed during the Lost Wars, they took advantage of a clause in their Tir-noNog's laws and increased their control. Unlike her father and mother, Queen Mab, Titania is a figurehead controlled by their whims and wants nothing to do with them.

"Besides, if I send her off to Gen, we'll have an insider."

"And you think she would comply? Do you know her?"

"She'll learn to deal with males sooner or later. Clausa can't hurt a Diptera; she'll run circles around him."

"She is not like you, Titania."

"They won't hurt her. As barbaric as Gentiana is, he's the one who pitched the idea."

"He is the Elf that blew away a whole kingdom. You're telling me him having her doesn't worry you?"

"Why should it? Gen needs her alive, and I'm sure one of those Buzzards already offered her up for security. They know what's coming."

Titania rolled her eye right before she drained the bottle into her mouth. She knew Anemone wasn't ready, but serving under Gentiana would keep her safe and give her experience. The more she thought about it, the surer she was. Someone else put the idea into Gentiana's mind. Gentiana was a schemer, but he was more vicious than that. He would have taken her without the peace charade if he needed Anemone that bad. Regardless Albion would be safer than Tir-noNog, and the sooner she could keep Anemone away from here, the better. If Anemone were anything like Titania, she would understand the duty of doing so.

"Tell me, Florentina, what have they done with those inflicted with *KleptOdmania*?"

Florentina sighed. "Just as you would expect. The Od-less are locked out in the Mars Ruins."

"The Salt mines? Do you think it has to do with the Lost Tech graveyard? Any more updates on their condition?"

"I'm not sure, and besides the lifeless eyes and Od sapping, they're starting to develop crystal-like skin."

"This gets stranger and stranger. There's a reason they're stowing them out there. They don't spread like wildfire from a simple tap; something doesn't sit well with me."

"If I had to guess, they know not a soul would wander out there."

"True, but I doubt they're doing it to contain the problem. I'm worried about these boots on the streets."

"I could not agree with you more."

It was one of the many reasons Titania hesitated to increase Phloem Guard patrols throughout Tir-noNog. With Gallu-Utukku and Therianthrope's power growing, she knew they had to keep the kingdom strong. But she also understood more troops on the street caused fear. If they weren't careful, one Aos-Si with *KleptOdmania* could become a group, but the process for *KleptOdmania* took longer.

Rather than staying behind walls and negotiating policies, fighting was her blood. She saw that passion in Anemone's eyes, and it often struck Titania with fear. Titania wanted Anemone as far away from the battlefield as possible. Titania tried many times to convince Anemone to stay behind the walls, and she felt Anemone was far more inclined to politics and negotiations than she was. It was one of the reasons she did not hesitate on Anemone's wedding to Clausa.

Titania could feel it in her aching bones. Something was occurring behind closed doors in *that* kingdom. Albion was perfect on paper, and having Anemone as a liaison between the two domains would work in Tir-noNog's favor. Also, she fears the worst with the barrier. Checking the sigil on her left arm, she could see its connection was weakening. It would be some time before it fell, but the presence of its fall loomed in her mind. Nothing would protect them from *him* when that barrier fell. A world without any means to stop *him* had no future. Her body shivered, trying to perish the idea of his arrival. That happening often crippled her, but she worked through it. Gentiana was a fool, but he was not foolish enough to do anything too rash, so she hoped.

"Florentina, has anyone found more information on Vestri?"

"The Dwarven king?" Florentina questioned. "No. You still think it had something to do with Albion?"

Titania laughed. "I know it does, and it's why I've been excavating Alberich, and I found something connected to Albion."

"Oh?" She responded, "What might that be?"

"The remnants of the entire kingdom had become a ghost town. A whole kingdom doesn't just disappear without warning."

"After that blast and the embargo, there wasn't much reason for them to stay. Couldn't the rest of the kingdom have moved out?"

"No, that's too many unaccounted for, and the blast was near the edge of their wall. Not to mention there were *sigil*s in the city's sewer system. Ones I had never seen before except in two places."

"I suppose one of them was Albion, and the other was old Tir-noNog?"

Titania scoffed, "I don't care how great Gentiana *knows* he is. I sense foul play, something like Lost Ars. Something that involves Mehen."

"Do you think he knows about the lantern?"

"There's not a chance in Muspell he'll know where I hid it."

Suddenly Titania was taken aback by that statement. When she thought about it, Florentina would know nothing about *that* lantern. After all, she wasn't there when they had used it. Titania thought it was the alcohol messing with her mind for a moment. After she took another swig from her bottle and smelled a different aroma near the bottom of the mug, it was a somewhat subtle bitter smell. She wiped her finger along the bottom of the cup and noticed a purple film. It was different from the deep red from the Currants occasionally added to the Pear blended mead.

There was a tingling sensation slowly trickling through her body. She was so focused on her fingers that Titania hadn't realized Florentina had stopped talking. When she turned to tell her how tired and confused, she felt someone else was standing in her place. Her vision was blurred, but Titania noticed a pendant they wore. It was a familiar one she could never forget, no matter how much she tried. She quickly drew her blade, but its weight made her stumble.

"That belonged to Fokker before Gen—" Titania leaned on her sword.

"I know it did just like *she* did," the voice hissed.

Titania raised her blade and struck at them, but they parried her strike with their Sword-Breaker. As the blade slid down, Titania threw a backhand at their face. Her movements were so sluggishly they used the same weapon to slap her hand away, barely nicking the back of her hand. Quickly they grabbed Titania by the throat and tossed her onto her bed like a doll. A soft voice spoke as they dangled a small vial over Titania's head.

"You're not the only one I cooked this batch up for, and now that I have your attention, I'll need you to extend the prep for your little trials."

"Who are you?" Those words weakly left Titania.

"I know puppets were more my thing but hush. No questions asked." They raised their finger to her lips. "It's all for Nin."

Before she closed her eyes, a shadow flew into her room. Quickly the stranger took on Titania's form, and the shadow covered her vision. The world's color faded as she felt their hand cover her face.

REVELATIONS AT HAND

My memories jumped again, and I saw a blurry scene in front of me. We were in Tir-noNog as her body lay before me in a pool of blood. Emotion began to swell in my chest, and my breathing grew erratic. Soon I could see the scene much clearer. I had pierced her chest, holding her beating heart in my hand. As Titania's hand grazed my face, she whispered something into my ear, "Don't let her forget Spriggan or me." The Transcendent looked at me as if I had spoken those words aloud. I turned my head, and another memory popped into my mind like whiplash. This time it was Spriggan, and he asked me about someone named *Belladonna*.

By the Transcendent shoving another one of the fruits in my face, she instantly ruined my train of thought. My eyes darted at her with frustration. Strangely enough, she seemed to have become far less threatening. The look on her face was so docile I couldn't help but relax my face.

"You are totally ruinin' my internal monologs right now."

"Good, because I somehow feel offended by the word *docile*."

"I'm sorry. Say what now?"

"Your thinking is too loud!"

"Come again? You can hear my thoughts?"

"There's almost no such thing as thoughts here, you dolt. In here, you are your thoughts."

"Oh, you're just telling me this now!?"

"You didn't ask. Have you seen me open my mouth this entire time?" She pouted.

Calling her a smartass seemed like a bad idea since she could read my mind and crush me like an Insecta. Oddly, I had almost forgotten what an Insecta was; somehow, it reminded me of her. When I looked at her arms, they became practically plated like an Insecta, and now she even had antennae and wings.

"I can still hear you."

"I still don't care!"

As if under her breath, "Friggin dolt."

But she was right. I assumed she was talking this whole time conventionally, but that wasn't the case. I could hear her words without her lips moving. Seeing how I embodied my thoughts could explain how losing my sense of self affected my form. If that was the case, why did she still have her form? What made her retain her shape, and how did she look at herself?

"A freak with power who was too weak to do anything."

She had answered without my uttering. Her facial expressions didn't change much, but I could hear her voice shifting. The tone in her voice was beginning to rise and fall. It was no longer dry, and it seemed she was becoming more expressive now. Something must have resonated with her from her words and how her facial expression had slightly changed from her usual neutral expression. However, there was still a somber look on her face. Instead of the usual predator-like focus, her eyes had softness; she had even begun to blink.

The Transcendent no longer had this overwhelming presence. Instead, she resembled a child. She tucked her head into her knees and held her legs close to her body as she sat still. I could see my hand reaching out to her, but I stopped. The situation made me uneasy, not because of fear but concern. I genuinely didn't know if I should pry or not. Although I didn't have my memories, my gut told me correctly consoling anyone was beyond my skills. Since this was a timeless realm that trapped our Transcendent, she topped that list of "unhelpable."

Suddenly she plopped to her side without untucking her knees. It was like watching someone tipping a doll over. Her body hardly reacted to hitting the tree. Even though the absurdity of her not responding to her fall made me want to laugh, I felt terrible for her. Then another thought popped into my mind. If this was how she viewed herself, I wondered what she looked like before. Seeing as she said, everyone in the fruits felt familiar. She must be one of the Aos-Si seen in them. As she seemed relatively young, it had to be Anemone. The more I thought about it more similarities I saw in their features. The only significant difference was jet-black skin and long, wavy silver hair. Hell, even their eyes were similar colors.

Her chains rose, grabbing onto the five fruits she had picked and dropped them near her lap. She was perfectly still and looked like she was reflecting on my question. Before I asked another question, she spoke up.

"I don't want to be her."

I annoyingly responded, "Quit reading my mind. Also, why not?"

There was a long pause before she rolled to her other side, facing away from me.

"She's annoying and isn't honest about how she feels."

Some of me found it difficult for her not to believe that was her. Then again, there were still three more for me to see. Instead of making my official choice now, seeing the rest might be a good idea. I looked back into Rubus and Anemone's fruit but saw nothing. To be exact, I saw fog and blurred images.

"Are these things broken or?"

"No, you dolt! Didn't you hear me tell you the linked Memoria?"

"Come again? Also, when?"

"Ugh...To see more, you have to look at the Vitis in order of events of relevance. You can't see what comes next without the context of what led up to those moments."

"What kinda convoluted LS?"

"I didn't make the friggin rules. Would you rather watch the entirety of a lifetime and then go back and piece it all together? Just be grateful you didn't have to learn it on your efforts."

"Fair... Also, own efforts?"

My eyes darted at the scenery of endless trees and fruits, only to land back on here. If what was said was true, the Transcendent saw all of these damn things in order. That idea was almost mind-numbing. How did she stand doing such a thing? If she had scrolled through thousand or more of these trees, it was no wonder she didn't know who she was! Having an identity crisis, in hindsight, could easily make someone reject themselves. Only the heavens knew how long she had been here.

"Don't be absurd. I didn't see every single one, just those relevant to my Memoria."

"Well... How long or how many did you go through to get to this tree?"

"I lost count after a thousand. I lost my sanity after only ten."

"Is that hyperbole?"

She avoided my eye contact. It made me wonder if it took only ten of them to lose their mind. I don't know if that's good or bad but experiencing ten different lives was still impressive. Just jumping through these four was hard to decipher if I was one of them. I sat next to her recalling when I touched that tree and how it surged those lives through me. When I unconsciously summoned my Adnero, it protected me. Had it not covered my body, I wondered what would have happened to me.

"How are you coping in this place? If it were me, I would have smashed my head already."

"I already tried that. Volition won't let me die, and to be honest, I don't even know if I can die again."

"Volition?"

Her hand pointed towards the chains that floated around. Looking at them sent shivers down my spine. As they continued to rattle in the background, the sound echoed in my mind. Another memory of Anemone flashed in my mind. She was younger than the Queen but a bit older than she was in the Vitis fruit. Strangely enough, her eyes resembled a green color instead of her usual fuchsia, and she wore a bell in her hair. It was the dead of night, and her arm was bleeding. Even with tears rolling down her face, she held a blade. I was on the floor, and it looked like she was protecting me from something, but fire and smoke obscured my vision.

My eyes slid across the surrounding area in ruins. Someone attacked Tir-noNog, but I couldn't remember why. I couldn't see it clearly, but my body knew it was there. Anemone raised her blades and launched a volley of Volition into the smoke. My eyes flickered as my fuzzy sight tried to stay focused. Instantly the vision disappeared, and the Sillih Caudex returned in front of me. The view of her controlling those chains seemed contradictory. How could she control them then but not now?

"Are you sure you can't control them?"

"No, the chains are far too fickle for my control. I never learned even when I was alive, which was one of my regrets."

Her gaze held wordlessly on the fruits. Even though she stopped there, never trying to describe that "regret," her face said it. I could tell she didn't want to explore those feelings anymore. Before I could ask her about anything else, she shoved two other fruits in my face. Placing the other two down, I grabbed them. I didn't know if it was a good idea, but I figured I'd still ask a bit more instead of looking into them.

"What else do you remember about your life? If you say everyone seems familiar, that's a start. Do you remember anything about a Fog mask and a robed figure?"

"Fog mask? No, but I remember hating Acaulis and hating Gentiana even more."

"Gentiana?"

For her to bring up his name felt off-putting for some reason. Who was he, and why did everyone want him dead? His presence was like a chain that connected everyone. Both his sons wanted him gone, and so did Titania and Spriggan. Everyone mentioned him, and his efforts to bring peace to the world may have been a charade. His connection to Spriggan seemed vengeance-filled, and Titania had her distrust. Although my gut aligned with their thoughts, there was more to it, even if I couldn't put my finger on it. The scene of me lying beneath the rubble from that explosion appeared again, and I saw an elf with long flowing hair wearing the mask Rubus saw. It made me wonder who that shadowy figure appeared in the background and if it was Gentiana.

"Who is Gentiana exactly?"

"Depending on who you ask, a hero or villain."

"Ah, one of those depending on which side of history situation."

"He's the mastermind that helped hunt your kind."

"My kind? What do you mean?"

"You're a Denizen, aren't you?"

The word "Denizen" resounded inside me; it's what Aos-Si called us. Something told me we called ourselves something different. We were the keepers of the sacred flames, the original wielders of Adnero; it was one of the first lessons *she* taught me. Since we crossed paths, Aos-Si coveted our ability to manifest things into reality. Or at least that's what my master told me. Right after that realization, a laid-back, whimsical voice scoffed dryly. I often heard that I both loved and hated it more than the inevitable cold of winter. I could hear her say, "Get brave! Or you'll never get far in life!"

After that, a sharp-pitched sound pierced my ears and forced my eyes to widen. I adjusted my jaw and felt its cracking as I tried to get my hearing back to normal. As I looked at the Transcendent talking, I could only assume I was out of it the whole time, and I couldn't hear a thing since my mind was out of it.

"In the end, Gentiana was the *mighty* hero who saved Abhainn-Reatha, or so the story goes."

"Is that so?"

"I'm guessing you weren't listening. You look like Muspell."

"Sorry, but my memories are coming in and out. It's seriously throwing me off."

More memories resurged, and I heard the Red-headed Fae explaining three types of Adnero. However, that drilling sensation in my head from earlier quickly cut off her explanation. Soon after, the name *Mehen* popped into my mind. It was a name Titania had mentioned in that dream, but it didn't stick out before. My mind spun as inaudible scenes of her talking to me crossed my vision back and forth.

"Are you drilling into my mind again!?" I glared.

"I didn't drill into your head."

"Now you're just screwing with me."

"No, I'm not. I was sitting here the whole time and handed you the fruits."

My mind felt warped; there was no way I had imagined that. As our eyes stayed locked, her face had a genuine look of confusion. Whether it was my imagination or not, it didn't change the fact it felt unnatural. She tossed Anemone's Memoria into my hands, and I caught it.

"This should be accessible now."

"Sheesh, you're pushy."

"You try being stuck here for a thousand lifetimes and see how fast you want to leave. If there's any chance of helping, you can get me out of here. I'll gladly do so."

"And you're sure I'm your ticket out of here."

She glared at me and then turned away. "You better be...."

Her face softened, and her body slumped into a puddle.

"You *really* are like *her*.

I said those things, yet I didn't know why. After all, I didn't even know who *she* was. Suddenly one of her chains launched Anemone's Vitis into my face, and it slammed into my mouth. As I bit into it, I saw

Anemone's Memoria. But this time, I could even see her dream, and it was a place I knew I had seen before.

...Before the trials

A nemone stood inside something that resembled a temple. Her body moved on its own, running towards the large entrance. The sound of muffled screams echoed from outside, drawing her in closer. Even with the cries, her mind was clear, and her body was calm. A sea of black flames poured through the city's streets below when she stepped out. Her eyes lowered to those running up the stairs, and as their voices called, she couldn't understand a single word they said.

The holy temple stood in the city's epicenter, towering over nearby buildings. Its exterior walls blocked out the surrounding ocean of sand and kept the flames neatly tucked in the town. The inferno blended with the starry night sky as small golden lights twinkled in the dark fires. Every gold light had smaller orbs of either blue, red, yellow, or green orbiting them, but slowly they all dimmed in flames.

Warriors formed a defensive line at the stairs' bottom as the individuals scurried inside the temple. When she followed the citizens back through the entrance, a man dazzled in golden armor spoke to her. The golden man's hand grabbed her shoulder and pushed her to the side as someone in a hooded robe lunged past her. She regained her footing quickly, but they stood in front of her again. Their arms stretched in front of her face, and rattling chains echoed. She stared into the black fire spouted from their hands, and her mind went blank. The same flames that burned through the city gave her a deep feeling of emptiness: a horrifyingly cold feeling, and every sense of fear dissipated into sheer apathy.

When Anemone's eye flashed open, she noticed her body was covered in sweat. She couldn't even scream in fear as she shuddered. The weight of her body made her buckle when she tried to sit up. Anemone raised both her arms and looked at the scars under her sigils.

Her left fist clenched her bed as she placed her other arm over her eyes. All she could do was continue to take deep breaths and calm herself.

"Really? All this over a nightmare? I'm so pathetic."

It wasn't the first time she had nightmares of strange places she had never been. These dreams had been going on for some time, and she didn't know what to make of them. That city in the desert was a reoccurring part of her dreams; in it, she had seen many unfamiliar faces. This time the nightmare felt far more accurate than the others.

"Black fire... I've never heard of such a thing," Anemone whispered.

The flames didn't even emit heat, leaving an eerie sensation in Anemone's mind. It was so traumatizing it left her legs feeling weak. Just trying to swing her legs off her bed exhausted her. As she sat up again, sunlight from outside caught her eye and told her it was morning. The last time she looked out, dawn was on the verge of occurring. It seemed she had tossed and turned until late, and when she finally fell asleep, she had a nightmare. When she finally got the strength to get out of bed, her mood only dropped more. Even though she should have been excited for today, her body left her with no room for positivity. She rolled onto the floor and got dressed on the ground.

The four-day festival was on its last day, and the road stayed filled with foreign vendors clearing their stalls. Anemone feigned, listening to Spriggan as they strolled through the main road. He drilled her with questions that would be on the written exam. While Spriggan prepared her on combat strategies and Flux theory questions, a sudden chopping sound made Anemone's body jump. Quickly her eyes darted behind her, and she saw a butcher lob off the head of a Ragifer carcass. Her eyes widened, and her mind replayed the scene of that Elf from yesterday. The smell of flesh made her want to hurl. Spriggan stared at her and stopped talking about Od and its applications in combat.

"You look like your worlds come crashing down. Was it your mother?"

Trying to fake strength, she shrugged her shoulders.

"You nailed it. I didn't get much sleep thanks to last night's discussion with Titania and another nightmare."

"Those things are starting to get worst. Was it as bad as learning you are betrothed to Clausa?"

"You knew?" She huffed.

"If I had told you, you would be sulking as you are now."

Anemone was mad that she knew he was right, but she could hardly cope with her feelings. She clenched her fist and took a deep breath to channel the Arcane Od around her. Slowly her body calmed down. It felt like she was wasting her Od to center herself, but it was worth it if she wore her feelings.

"About that dream... was it the one with the Desert kingdom?"

She nodded her head in silence. No one had any idea why she saw these dreams. Florentina assumed they might be visions of some sort, but there weren't any known kingdoms in the desert. None of the books in Tir-noNog's libraries have much info on the Arid Seas and the temple's geography, which might be its location. Then again, the Wildlands were relatively unexplored territory. Some maps had travel routes sketched, but it was too treacherous for any normal Cartographer.

Even nomads who had crossed it did their best to avoid unnecessarily long excursions. Anemone couldn't imagine that she could have reason to have vision anyway. Titania never had psychic foresight to something as pre-ordained, so why would she? Anemone crossed her arms as she remained in thought. When she recalled the comments of the mob last night and her discussion with her mother, her chest swelled. Any good news would make her day at this moment. If there was any chance to understand her dreams and why she became cursed without Elemental Od, maybe it involved her father.

"Spriggan?"

"Yes?"

The two stopped walking and stared at each other, dead in the eyes. Even though Anemone wanted to have this conversation, the timing was lousy. She was so excited before but knew anything more emotional than yesterday's news might belabor her focus. The dreams had been unexplainable for a long time, but something was nagging at her more than ever.

Besides Quarz bringing up the topic, the identity of her father was something that had escaped her until now. Her memory played a scene of her first attempt as a child. Back then, Titania gave her the cold shoulder and told Anemone, "Don't worry about him; just worry about yourself." After that, Anemone never found the courage to bring it up again. She had constantly seen the same golden-armored, long-haired man in her dreams and wondered if there was a connection to her. Knowing that Titania would not give her that information, she needed to get it off her chest.

"Do you know about my father? I know I've never asked, but...."

"Quarz mentioned him, didn't he?"

Anemone nodded her head, and he stroked his beard. His hand reached for the dagger he always had at his side.

"I see there's a lot on your mind."

When Spriggan turned around, he had a troubled look as they realized their stroll had gotten them close to the test facility. Before he said anything, Aronia had crept from behind and wrapped her arms around Anemone. She had startled Anemone, and when Aronia saw the look on her face, she could tell she was in a bad mood. Aronia stood there puzzled since she seldom saw Anemone openly express distress. Aronia placed her hand on Anemone and threw a thumbs-up.

"I dunnae why yer in a rut, but don't you wurry. I've got yer back. Glum or not."

Anemone smiled wirily. "What would I do without you?"

"Be alone?"

"I wasn't hoping for honesty, y'know."

Anemone having Aronia's positive energy forced a smile on her face. Spriggan also smiled and talked about their fate to befriend one another. Soon Spriggan's face grew grave as he turned to Anemone and pulled out the curved dagger he always carried. Spriggan carried that blade with him even if he had never used it. Anemone's eye looked at the knife and rolled back to him. She was confused as to why he would be giving it to her. He would never let her unsheathe or swing it around as a child, only holding the curved weapon in her hand. Long ago, he said it belonged to his son Fokker, who was also skilled in Arcane Ars like Anemone was. She had heard a few stories of him here and there, but Spriggan almost avoided talking about him.

"This Kukri belonged to your father. Who was like a son to me."

At this very moment, Anemone concluded that Fokker was her father. From a young age, knives felt far more natural to her, even when training to use polearms and bows. She took the knife from him and held it tight. A fine hide with a silken tassel wrapped the handle and sheath of the Kukri. The moment she unwrapped it, she unsheathed it and stared at the craftsmanship of the blade. In Spriggan's hands, it looked like a knife, but as she held it again, it was as large as a short sword. The blade was almost as long as her forearm. What stuck out more was the waves resembling meshed earth layers running from its base to its tip. It was like no metal she had ever seen before. Anemone rubbed her fingers across its smooth sides and felt no indentations. Something about this knife felt more sentimental than she could imagine. Spriggan placed his hand on her head to console her.

"I'm proud of you, Sprout. No matter what, I'm sure Titania is too. Forget about what she said."

"I know... but that's not—"

"Don't worry," he interrupted. "When you finish with the trials, we'll finish this conversation. Although Titania should, I'll tell you about everything, including your father."

At first, Anemone thought he would derail the conversation and tell her nothing. He was always an Aos-Si of his word, so she knew he would say to her what she wanted. Instead, Spriggan put her worries to ease in only a few sentences. She flung her arms around Spriggan and squeezed him as she fought the tears from her eyes.

"What about Titania? Won't she be mad at you or me for wanting to know?"

"Forgive her even if she is. We've kept so much from you for reasons we thought would protect you." Spriggan grabbed her shoulder, spun her around, and gently pushed her forward, "For now, think only of the trials and nothing else. We will talk more afterward."

Anemone huffed and clenched her arm as she wiped her tears. She looked around to see if anyone was looking, but they were focused more on their destinations. Even after hearing what Spriggan said, she still worried about Titania. If his telling her anything would affect his relationship with Titania, she didn't want that. Besides Aronia, it felt like he was her only family.

On the other hand, Titania chose to be gone more times than she could count. That aside, a part of Anemone still wanted affirmation from Titania. She was competing in an important event to prove her worthiness as a leader, but Titania was far more focused on the bigger picture. She was always worried about the greater good of everyone else. It never seemed like her mother looked at her as much as she tried. Competing in the Accolade Trials was frightening, but she knew Titania had also participated. For years she waited for the moment to prove she could be just as great as her. Aronia placed her hand on her back, and the two of them waved as he left, and they continued to the facility. Aronia turned to Anemone and pinched her cheek.

"I won't pull it out of Ye. Just tell me later. But now's not the time for sadness, missy. Hop to yer feet and move! We have the challenge to conquer," Aronia shouted.

Anemone gave her a thumbs-up, and she reciprocated. In times like this having her around was perfect. Aronia always pulled her up and kept her going, no matter how she felt. Having her stand next to her gave her the boost she needed. During their walk toward the facility, the sensation of countless eyes made Anemone's skin crawl. No one commented, but they turned away every time she attempted to make eye contact. As the Queen's daughter, many believed she used that to earn her rank and get into the Arbor Magna.

They weren't entirely wrong since she was royalty, but alongside her mother's lack of expectations, it wasn't an easy time for her. The traditional way to join the Arbor Magna was to be at the top of your primary academy and get a recommendation from a Commanding Officer. A CO would assign an obscure task that the Council of Nine approved in the Kingdom's Embassy. All jobs varied from shadowing official surveys to assisting citizens in Tir-noNog. They were things you would do once you were of official rank in the Arbor Magna; only you had chaperones.

After entering the facility, she saw a poster showing the Arbor Magna branches, the Lance Thorn Force, the Phloem Guard, and Anthers Scouts. Many wanted to join the Arbor Magna to join Tir-noNog's military police, the Phloem Guard Force. It was common to mock the Phloem Guards since they stayed comfy guarding the inner walls of the kingdom and its Transportation Gates. The Anthers, on the other hand, covered anything past the borders. Initially, they traveled along with the Lance Thorns, providing conflict aid, language diversity, and recon during wartime. Nowadays, they aid in assisting recovering villages or supporting foreign affairs. She stood there and placed her hand on the Anthers, but maybe being in the Phloem Guard wasn't a bad option. As Aronia nudged Anemone, her mind came back into focus.

"Now I said what I did, but why do you look like someone burned away yer dreams?"

"Sorry, Nia. I just need a moment."

"Sorry, won't cut it now. All the paired seats are gone."

As Aronia left for the nearest seat, Anemone noticed how crowded the testing area was. She could tell there were at least a hundred trainees from a glance. There were seats available, but none were side by side. When she walked away, she saw Aronia talking to a classmate she had. As quickly as they came together, the two separated soon. Seeing Aronia with someone else made an unfamiliar feeling swell in her chest. The moment Aronia smiled, Anemone quickly turned her head.

"No distractions. I'll deal with that later."

Anemone slapped her cheeks and quickly looked for an available seat. Once this exam was over and she had more time, she promised to dissect her feelings later. After a few moments of searching, she sat near the middle of the central row. From the corner of her eye, she saw someone with familiar wavy brown hair with their head down. After turning, they raised their head, and she realized she had unexpectedly sat next to Rubus. An exasperated huff left her mouth as her eyes rolled. Slowly she turned her head, trying to avoid eye contact.

"If it isn't Wingless?" he yawned.

She kept her eyes forward, "If it isn't last night's punching bag? Can't you be more original?"

"Ouch, I felt that sting a bit." He leaned back into his chair.

"I doubt it. What do you want?" Anemone's head leaned into her arm.

"Aren't you the one who sat next to me?

"There aren't many seats left."

"Sheesh. I was hoping you were gracing me with the opportunity to thank you for last night."

Her eyes sharpened. "I honestly can't tell if you're genuine, Rubus."

"I am, but you and I both know that's not the entire point of this convo," he agreed.

Anemone rolled her eyes. "Fine. I'll humor you."

Rubus's aloof face disappeared, and his eyes focused on hers. They rarely made eye contact in most cases, but the look of intent sent a shiver down her spine.

"Do you know what an Eidolon is?" he asked.

She thought his question was pointless at first, but it could have been on the exam, so she gave him the benefit of the doubt.

"A fairy tale from the time of yore. Beings who can channel the form and powers of Celestials. Why ask?"

"I don't think they are fairytales," he said, "Call me a fool if you'd like, but I think there's another one in TirNog, and I'm hoping you can help me find them."

Anemone groaned as she turned away from him in her seat. He dared to ask her for a favor after his actions last night and for such an unreasonable request. Celestials were long gone, and many forgotten. The tall tales and the belief of the Sacred Trio were the only reason anyone believed they were once actual. Even they hadn't been seen in over a century. Anemone felt foolish trying to entertain him, and the urge to avoid him heightened. She was tired of him appearing in her background. Ever since they crossed paths with each other, there has been conflicting. They were like Were-felid and Lycanthropes, natural enemies. Instead of calling him out for wasting her time, she promised to ignore him for the rest of the test.

Once everyone finished sitting, the assistants were already handing out tests. The proctor gave a long speech about what to expect from the test. Everyone had two hours to finish all four sections. Anemone already knew the most extended section was the Bestiary section. It emphasized understanding the Flora and Fauna, the tactics needed to deal with them, and their use. The other three were Weapons, Equipment, and Maintenance, Combat and Scenario tactics, and Flux Theory, which Anemone found most straightforward.

The proctor told the class to finish by any means necessary during the period. Spriggan had already warned her that cheating was technically allowed with a small caveat. Anyone caught cheating would be excused and automatically fail. The amount of info jammed into the test was overwhelming on purpose. The whole point was to make everyone mentally exhausted to be at their wits' end when they did the infield exam. She wasn't worried about cheating since she had been cramming everything into her head and already had a plan. Even if she was under the weather, answering the questions was no problem.

Before they began, the proctor had one last explanation about the infield part of the Trials. During the Trials, Comrade-at-Arms for the Arbor Magna Military took tactics, survival readiness, and spell-casting tests. Teams would be sent into the wilderness of Tir-noNog's woods and given tasks to complete. Those tasks varied from retrieving a particular item to securing a location from mock enemies or hunting a specific creature. If they succeeded, examinees would get promoted to Corporal.

When the proctor finished, they told everyone to begin. Anemone instantly skipped the Bestiary and went straight to Flux theory since it was her best subject. As she looked at the exam, none of the questions for that section were that difficult, and they were simple questions based on the Od combination.

"If there is no hydro-aloe for burns, what Ars would you cast and what Flux(s) of Od could synthesize the proper Ars?"

Usually, hydro-aloe use while channeling Arcane Od to increase physical regeneration was the go-to option. If you didn't have a Synergist to do so, you had other options. If your Flux had Undine Od mixing it with Arcane Od would cast Hydrotherapy. If you didn't have Undine, you could also mix Arcane and Vulcan for a Heat-Redux, weakening the Burn and reducing the effect of Vulcan-Ars that the recipient would receive. Knowing how one's Flux split helped the user understand their limit to cast Ars. It was a simple matter of knowing your Flux and mixing Od to synthesize the proper Ars creatively. Of course, it was more technical than that, but it was a simple enough answer.

Thinking about Flux variation, Anemone began to remember the traditional affinities in times of yore. Fae represented the Eastern woods and was traditionally known for Sylph. The Dwarves of the northern mountains for Oread, Nymphs of western seas for Undine, Ellylldan of the southern dry lagoons for Vulcan, and Elves of the central prairies for Arcane. As times changed, so did everyone's Flux. Even if they weren't Demi-breeds, differing Aos-Si were born with Elemental Od different from their race. Thanks to elemental diversity, many roamed for masters of differing Od, leaving their homelands searching for mastery. It was the start of cultural mixings and more changes in Flux configuration. Lucky for her, the next question was relevant and relatively straightforward, even with a follow-up response.

"List multiple Flux configurations and Secondary Elemental Ars that a Multi-Flux Wielder may have or produce. What are the flaws of Non-Pure Flux?"

Mono and Dual split were typical among younger Aos-Si thanks to cultural mixing. What was rarer was someone born with Tri-Flux or Quad-Flux. Even if one's Flux could connect to all four elementals, it didn't mean you could use them simultaneously. Using Oread, Sylph, Undine, and Vulcan Od was almost improbable but possible. In most cases, someone's Flux was more connected to one or more elements than another. That meant there was a firm limit on the amount of Ars you could cast of a particular elemental Od.

Multi-flux users often struggled to channel enough secondary Od for a spell. Few Multi-Flux wielders could create secondary elements like Chione, Wolfram, or Taranis, but it wasn't always the case. Besides the droughts affecting Od, Dual-Flux wielders and above generally struggled to do higher-tier magic. The higher the tier of Ars cast, the more powerful and taxing it was on your Flux. Excluding Lost-Ars or spells past the Fifth tier, the average Pure-Flux could cast the Fourth tier without significant fatigue.

The lack of fatigue was something Anemone was somewhat proud to have. Although everyone understood that almost anyone could use Arcane, not everyone could be proficient in using it. Naturally, some were far more gifted in using it than others, giving rise to the importance of Synergist and Saboteur Ars. Acting as support, they either boosted the strength of those around them or weakened those opposing them.

The section ended on knowing which spells belonged on what Ars tiers, casting methods, and the history of spells. The history of magic was the most useless information to know. Before Lumenopal and Grimoires, everyone used to do Full Casts or Scribing Ars as in an ancient tongue of a long-forgotten origin. Modern equations for casting formatted Ars as; Od-Size: Tier: Spell-(Target), for example, "Vulcan-Gigas: 2ND Tier: Tyndre (Target)". After advancements in Ars's theories, they learned you only need to Scribe the Od Elemental Sigil, vocalize the spells name, and understand your target. Since everyone incorporated these formulas with Bestiary analysis for casting, Anemone studied this subject at least, if any.

It was a fundamental basis for casting Ars more effectively. Your spell could hone in as long as you know your target and can see them. Otherwise, the attack will fly in the direction your body or eyes pointed. Either way, you still had to confirm what the target was. Throughout her life, she could never get interested in Bestiary studies. She wasn't interested in animals, but sketching plants often caught her attention.

The Bestiary section tested one's knowledge of the surrounding fauna and flora that posed a threat—knowing as much as possible about your opponent made or broke Ars offensively or defensively. Much like Aos-Si, there was fauna that could use Od. Albeit less gracefully, it was imperative to take their strength seriously. Most only used mild forms of Arcane, but rare species used elemental Od. Those species later inspired the basis for Elemancy, the equipping of element qualities on your weapons. Some beings had natural affinities for some elemental Od, making them resistant or nearly immune to Ars of the same association. After her thoughts ran on while she answered questions, a simple Bestiary question appeared.

"What beast is more likely to have either Vulcan or Chione?"

Anyone who knew anything about old war stories knew one of the answers was a Megaloceros. It was a large wooly elk with antlers the size of an Aos-Si. Depending on the region, their antlers could engulf fire or ice. Some affinities weren't as apparent for other Fauna or Therians, and one would have to use trial and error to strike for Od's vulnerability. The old tried and proper method of "Hitting it until it died" was your best bet for those without Od.

After an hour and a half, Anemone was on the last section involving weapon maintenance. All that was left was the other half of the Bestiary she skipped. Dread aside; there wasn't much time left to finish if she kept a steady pace. Suppose any question demanded too much time; she marked and skipped it for later. After thirty minutes, she completed the written exam and looked around.

As her eyes wandered, she realized a bit of Od in the air. It was faint, but she could tell others were using Ars during the exam. She was so focused on the exam she hadn't paid attention to it before. Anemone had forgotten to see if anyone had cheated, and to her surprise, there were empty seats. Either they got caught, or they finished before her. Anemone began to worry once she noticed the complete tunnel vision she had focusing on the exam—hopefully, she would be alert enough for the infield section.

Raising out of her chair, Anemone saw a green-haired elven male sitting with an unopen exam packet. The Elf seemed to have dozed off after not even finishing the first page. As she began to walk away, she saw his name written, "Rowan Sorbus." The only reason the name caught her attention was that she knew Rowan was the Genus name of Sorbus. The young Elf's name was technically Rowan-Rowan. The play of words on his name made her chuckle a bit. After she walked to the front of the room and turned in her booklet, she looked to see if Rubus was still doing his exam.

Anemone forced a smirk on her face having finished before him. Her smugness caught his eye as she walked out, but he sighed and shrugged his shoulders. Regardless of his reaction, she considered it her win. The whole time they had shared class, he never had a higher score than her. She already knew there wasn't a chance in Muspelheim he would beat her today. Distraught or not.

...Changes, Luck, and Variety

A nemone sat near the exit of the facility awaiting Aronia to come out. It was frustrating to know they wouldn't receive their written exam results until they returned from the infield exam. The goal was not to hamper the participating Comrade-at-arms' morale as they approached the second half of the exam. As confident as she was, she wanted to know how well she did. Instead of dwelling on her results, she took this time to rest for another moment. Suddenly a peculiar sensation left her mind feeling foggy as she closed her eyes. Her body broke into a cold sweat, and her legs felt like they were dragging through burning sand.

The level of lethargy that arose was terrible. Trying to channel Arcane Od to calm herself sent a sharp pain piercing through her head, forcing her eyes closed. When her eyes opened, there was a moment one of her eyes was seeing colorful flames near the center of everyone's chest. The bright flames were similar to those she saw in this morning's dream. When she was younger, she didn't experience anything peculiar like this—the only thing was those dreams. But the fact that channeling Arcane became difficult for her was absurd.

"What's going on with my body," she thought.

Anemone wouldn't let anything stop her from finishing the Accolade Trials, but her body was fighting her. Trying to keep calm, she covered her eye and continued focusing. Little by little, the tension in her head eased, and her body slowly calmed. Soon she saw the small colorful flames disappear, and the pain was relieved. As her eyes looked back at the ground, a pair of boots landed in her sight. Anemone saw Aronia extending a folded paper containing medicine.

"Looks like someone's finally in season."

"Maybe, or I'm just hungry," Anemone declined. "I'm surprised you still had some left."

Aronia dug in her bag and tossed a homemade meal bar at Anemone. "You're the one who made me a month's supply of Vitex mix. Remember, Succubae don't menstruate as often as Fae."

Anemone leaned on the wall behind her. "Hush, I genuinely doubt it's just that."

She paused, wondering if she would sound crazy for mentioning what was happening. She trusted Aronia, but there was immense uncertainty about what she was experiencing.

"Have you ever seen random colors floating around others?"

"Floatin' Colors? Like when Ye stare at the sun too long?" Aronia raised her brow, helping Anemone stand.

"No, never mind," she wobbled.

"What luck you've got getting so unwell before yer big day. Are Ye sure yer up for this, Luv?"

Anemone pumped her fist, "Trust me... I'm nowhere ready to back out."

As the two strolled forward, they walked towards the gathering Command-at-arms crowd. A thirty-minute window after the written exam finished allowed the participants to decompress. Judging from the crowd, it seemed like an even split of Albion and Tir-noNog recruits. They walked in between groups and overheard them talking about the exam and how they were either excited or deftly afraid. One of the convos that caught her attention was a group of Fae talking about increased Gallu presence. She overheard them say Gallu-Utukku sights in the forest have grown twice as much since the last trials, and stranger variations have appeared. Before hearing anything else, her mind played the scene from yesterday again. Her body tensed up as even the smell of blood flooded her senses. She turned her head to hide her displeased face from Aronia as she covered her mouth.

"It's shocking to see so many Femmes and Nues in the trenches," Aronia commented. "You'd think they all be too fearful."

"I don't think fear is something to consider. Don't you remember?"

Aronia nodded, "Oh yeah. I'd forgotten about the draft change since we were so Gung-ho about joining."

"Ever since the male population has plummeted, there's been an overhaul on many things. The Council wants more soldiers no matter who."

"A tale as old as time."

She heard most of the higher-ups discussing the ratio of soldiers. If it weren't for Albion's suggestion to join the Tir-noNog Accolade trials, female troops would have outnumbered the males. It was something she'd heard a few of the Commanding officers discussing. Many were worried about what would happen if all the young males died. But Anemone often believed they were too concerned about nothing. Children were born, so it's not like they'd run out of soldiers. Besides, Ars usually evened the odds between males, females, and intersex. If it wasn't for Anemone having at least Arcane Ars, there was no way Titania would have allowed Anemone to join the Arbor Magna. Spriggan's persuasion was also a bonus.

Although Anemone hadn't gone through the academy like everyone else, she had been training behind the scenes. Tutors handled most of her schooling, and Spriggan oversaw her combat training. Titania herself never thought it was an excellent idea for Anemone to join the academy, much less fight. She wanted her to be more academically inclined and avoid the battlefield. Anemone only assumed it was because Titania saw her as weak. From the moment the two of them had sparred with live weapons, Anemone knew. Titania struck her down without effort. Even after rushing Titania with a flurry of blows, Titania didn't take more than a few strikes to leave Anemone unarmed and with a broken will. Anemone could recall when Titania turned her back and said, "Without wings and sylph? That's what you have?" It took Spriggan and her tutor Hibernica to convince Titania that Anemone would be better off gaining more experience in the academy. Everyone thought she abused her royal authority to get here, but in her eyes, she worked hard.

To Titania's credit, Anemone was academically inclined, performing well above many of her counterparts. She may not have made it as a Liegeman, but her ability to use advanced Arcane Ars got her into a support class. When it came to live combat with her peers, she was pretty adept. Not top of the course, but she did what she could to compete with magic-slinging cadets. Regardless of her mother's and peer's disapproval, she wouldn't let that stop her from proving her worth. She would ignore their words and relish rubbing her high scores in their faces. After all this time of being called a runt and wingless, she could finally end their idiocy as a "Wingless Knight."

After a few moments of walking, a voice echoed from behind her and Aronia. She'd hope not to hear one until they were out in the wilds.

"If it isn't the Od-less Wingless, Princess Anemone."

"Of all the egos to speak their minds." Aronia sighed

"And what reason brings you here, Acaulis." Anemone turned around.

"Come now." Acaulis smiled crookedly. "You're not the only one of royal blood earning their stripes."

"Trying to beat Clausa, aye? Treaty children always have more to prove," Aronia mocked.

He stopped his hug and haughtily swayed his braided hair to reveal an elegant Sylph Lumenopal earring that pierced his ear.

"At least he's comparable... unlike you two." He paused. "And to think we are to become kin."

Anemone's eyes narrowed at the way he pointed his nose at them. It emanated an aura of arrogance and disgust, but who could blame him? If anyone had an inferiority complex, she knew it was him. Acaulis was born from a treaty to unite the Eastern and Western Albion kingdoms.

Clausa, on the other hand, was his firstborn and was consummated by an Elven woman he loved regardless of class. It wasn't even a well-known secret that he erred to the throne despite Clausa being born from a woman of lesser rank. Clausa had a far more welcoming personality, was a tremendous political figurehead, and had a cuter butt. No one could blame him for wanting to become a Cavalier to prove himself.

He stood in between them and placed his arms around their necks. "Don't worry. I won't make too many pleasantries with you."

"That's good, aye? Not like we wanted yer ego clouding up our air," jested Aronia

"No one asked for you to speak repugnant Demi vamp—."

Anemone cut him off. "Don't finish that sentence, Acaulis!"

His head tilted away from Anemone to side-eye her. "My apologies. I got sidetracked. I was hoping to congratulate you on your achievement. You were so close to becoming the second Wingless royal."

She glared daggers into his face. "Defamation of the Queen is a serious threat, Acaulis! I won't take that lightly."

"Now, let us not repeat the Black and Blue Crescent night."

"What do you mean?"

He chuckled. "Subitus Galinn."

Anemone looked at the ground, and a violent wind swirled, blowing her and Aronia into the air. Anemone covered her eyes instinctively as her body uncontrollably barreled into the air. Even while everything was spinning, she focused on an oncoming tree branch. After quickly shutting her eyes and drawing her sword breaker, she drove it into a tree branch near her. Casting Exalt: Xiphos during the impact, her arm bulked as its strength grew immensely. With the knife stuck into the side of the branch, her body spiraled around the stem, and she swiftly catapulted right back to the ground next to Acaulis.

"I hope I can learn to be as tactful as you." Anemone dusted her uniform off.

"And I hope your performance today blows me away and it stays cool," uttered Acaulis as he walked away

Anemone's chest slowly rose as the air that filled her heated up .to what was like a kettle, ready to burst. His words always sounded full of hot air, just like his puns were. Instead of exploding as she wanted, she let out a huff of air, only leering at him as he walked away. As much as she desired to retaliate now, Anemone knew all she had to do was wait. She knew tarnishing Tir-noNog's reputation with Albion over simple words wasn't worth it. If anything, they would settle their spat out in the wilds of the Dogger Lowlands or wherever they sent them out in the Seelie woods.

Aronia came down with her flapping her wings furiously. "How about ya blow me, ya royal—"

"Prick." Anemone smiled at Aronia as she folded her arms.

"What gives him the right to be so angry."

"Probably because he thought he was untouchable from the exile." Another voice caught her attention.

Anemone turned around and saw vaguely familiar green hair.

"And who might you be?"

"Rowan Sorbus, professional chef, and debt collector avoider. At your service."

Anemone had never met him before, yet he approached her with friendliness she had not experienced in some time. It was also a surprise to see someone who had done nothing on the exam be so chipper. She stepped back when she realized how close he was to her. He was already a strange Aos-Si, and she did not want to take chances.

"This may be a shocker, but Acaulis was antithetical to Albion's claim to be the purest Kingdom."

"How so?"

"If not for his status, he would have been exiled much earlier than other Od-less Elves."

"No way! Yer saying that bag of hot air is an Od-less?"

"Yup, but it's a secret, so don't tell anybody."

Rowan walked off with a wink and a wave. The wink from Rowan made Anemone gag, and Aronia laughed with her. Even though Anemone at least had Arcane Od, she was sympathetic about being looked down on. Anemone knew Albion had exiled those who didn't have control, but she didn't realize Acaulis was an Od-less. That only explained more of his petty nature. Titania had extended asylum to many who couldn't, but Tir-noNog lacked enough resources to take everyone. Only those with proof of trade or skill were allowed in. Their lack of Od made them expendable in the eyes of even some of Tir-noNog's citizens.

After a bit of time passed, everyone began assembling in groups and listening to the expected commemorative speech congratulating everyone's efforts for the first part of the exam. It was now the moment for team assignment to occur. Anemone couldn't help but pray that Acaulis wouldn't be on her team. She stared back at Aronia, thinking it would be an absolute dream to have the opportunity to beat Acaulis together.

However, Acaulis speaking of The Black and Blue Crescent caught her attention. The Black and Blue Crescent was the terror myth Titania's generation shared. When Anemone recalled it, everyone her age thought of it as an old horror fable to keep children in bed at night. "Under that blue moon, the streets burned with flames as blue as the moon-lit sky." Or so she heard.

As Anemone turned to Aronia to ask why Acaulis might have mentioned it, Aronia excused herself and headed back. Anemone looked back to see Aronia's running, but the crowd pushed her along. When the sea of Comrade-at-arms settled, Anemone found herself near the front of the group. A proctor stepped before the stage next to a large Lumenopal and explained the excursion.

"Your objectives remain simple; obtain an item, hunt a creature, or secure an individual back to a safe zone. Two teams of five will receive a letter for an assignment, and every two groups that share a letter will face the other rival team for the task. For example, team 1A would secure an individual while team 2A attempts to apprehend the individual."

After their speech, the Comrade-at-arms walked to the center of the stage, placed their hand on the large Arcane Lumenopal stone, and sent a pulse of their Arcane Od into the rock. Once everyone was finished, the stone shattered before their eyes. The proctor lifted one of them into the air and continued. Anemone recalled Spriggan telling her the Celestial's will would break into pieces equal to the number of contestants. It was also their will that the Lumenopal fragments could draw kindred spirits together.

"These shards will glow brighter as you get closer to your allies. The faster you assemble, the faster you may start."

In groups of five, everyone stepped forward and prepared to grab a fractured Lumenopal fragment. This test gauges their ability to feel the Od resonance pulling from their shards together. It was very straightforward, but Anemone realized something strange. The proctor said they were allowing a Lumenopal share to decide team synergy. This situation was acceptable beforehand, but this year's group comprised two different kingdoms.

"There's no way they want that," she muttered.

Judging from the sound of the crowd, it seemed she wasn't the only one who noticed. An even bigger air of restlessness arose from everyone. Everyone kept their heads straight, but brows raised, and mouths shifted. Once they started calling groups forward, Anemone was a part of the third group to step up. Her turn had come up, and she walked up the stairs to grab a Lumenopal shard. She fumbled around for a moment before deciding what shape to hold. It glowed bright and faded into a slight sparkle as she grabbed the fragment. Both she and the assistant stared at each other but said nothing. The assistant inspected the stone to ensure it wouldn't misfire, and after a bit, the assistant cleared her shard. It was strange for an Arcane fracture to sparkle that bright. Even though Anemone was superior to Arcane-Ars, she hadn't seen an Arcane Lumenopal shine like that.

Her eyes started acting up again as she walked back into the line. She saw the lights around at least half of the Aos-Si who stepped up. She saw more small, colorful balls floating around their center. This time, black, gold, or white flames were spinning at the top of their core, leading to a purple in the center. Some fires roared with an imbalance, while others were calm and in unison. Everyone seemed to have white, gold, or black combinations on top and a purple center, but the bases differed. When Aronia stepped up, her core had three red flames and one yellow at its base.

When Acaulis went up, she saw that his black fires were overpowering the white to the point it almost had disappeared. It almost mirrored the twisted smile he had crossing paths with Rubus, who had two cores. One had balanced white, gold, and black, but the other was chaotic. It had only black and gold with four colors flickering in and out—green was weaker, while yellow, blue, and red shined brighter. The moment Anemone rubbed her eyes, she could no longer see them.

It wasn't long until everyone stood back in line with a shard in hand, ready to go. The whole process took almost an hour, and everyone was on edge. Tension grew as everyone instantly prepared to assess each party member's strengths and weaknesses. None knew if the teams would be balanced out by skill or by the synergy of team composition. Hopefully, members would have basic coverage to compensate for adversity. But there was a chance you could end up on a team where everyone with similar Flux and perfect synergy. She only hoped someone on her team would support her because she wanted to play an aggressive role.

After one last speech, the proctor told everyone to find their teammates. When they saw their team, they would return to the stand and teleport to a location tied to the directive. At the sound of a whistle, everyone hurried to find the rest of their teams. Anemone could see the shard emitting four faint beams of purple light as if it drew the other fragments together. As Anemone stared at the chipped stone, she followed one of the steamers.

"Am I the only one who sees these?" She thought to herself.

The shard glowed brighter as she kept going forward. Since she was so focused on the light, she bumped into someone and quickly apologized. The piece shone more brilliantly, and she looked up. She stared at the tall Aos-Si, who towered over her. The Elf looked built like a tree trunk with a sturdy, stoic face to match his stature. His hair was short with a blond top and dark brown fade underneath. He raised his stone and responded with a deep voice.

"It seems you're on my team," he boomed. "I am Timber, from the eastern Albion region. It's a pleasure to meet you."

Anemone felt a slight twinge in her neck as she stared at him. When they raised their stones together, a rush of energy fused them. She was shocked by his stature since she had never seen someone so tall. Timber looked as if he ate metal as an appetizer. Knowing he couldn't be much older than her, she wondered how he got so big.

"It seems so," she responded.

He nodded, "Now, let us find the rest of our party."

Anemone nodded as she took his stone and followed him to the stream still flowing from the shard. After a while, her eyes stopped seeing the stream, but she pressed on. They crossed paths with Aronia and Rowan from earlier.

"Well, ain't this a miracle? Who'd guess we'd get paired?" Aronia Smiled.

"It's perfect," Anemone responded and smiled back. "Just glad I didn't get paired with Rubus or Acaulis."

"Why not? Aren't Ye in the mood to push boundaries?" Aronia chuckled.

"Ugh! Not in the least!"

While the two of them chatted, Timber and Rowan spoke to each other.

"Isn't this a team of reunions?" Rowan stated.

Timber nodded, "Indeed, all we need now is Ru."

"Looks like they know each other too," said Aronia.

"Me and this mountain Dwarf here had known each other before Albion's Academy transferred us. His dad was a personal artisan and merchant for the Sorbus family. Contrary to Timber's demeanor, he's got delicate hands." Rowan tapped Timber's shoulder.

"Dwarf? Aren't they endangered?" Aronia prodded.

"Half-elf, half-dwarf," Timber corrected. "But no, there's just so few of us left."

"Leave it to the Lost wars to decimate populations," Anemone continued.

"Another hybrid, aye," said Aronia, patting Timber on his back. "That's good on ya, lad!"

"So, we have a Succubae, a wingless Fae, and a living fossil. That's quite the combo."

Aronia tried to hide her surprise as she looked at Anemone. Anemone couldn't help but mutter her thoughts aloud.

"My luck is impeccable."

...Change of plans

To Anemone, Rubus was far better than Acaulis, but a stranger would have been even better! What should have been the start of her great adventure had slowly changed direction. She narrowed her brow as her eyes locked on Rubus. He quickly averted his eyes and turned his head away.

"Look, I don't have any interest in starting a fight with you," he exclaimed, turning his head.

"You say that, but we both know how this goes," Anemone hissed as she held back her urge to bicker.

"Yup, someone says something to rile up someone, and something happens, aye?" Aronia stepped between them and faced Anemone. "Nin, is this the time to start something?"

Anemone's eyes widened as her jaw dropped. "Why are you looking at me?" She raised her right arm and pointed at Rubus. "He is just as likely to start something!"

"In all fairness, I have *yet* to do anything."

"Yet!"

Anemone pointed at Rubus and signaled Aronia to agree with her. While they went back and forth, Timber and Rowan stood and observed the trio. Rowan tapped Timber's shoulders and non-verbally signaled his thoughts to him. He drew a heart with his hands with a smirk and a chuckle. Timber sighed, and before he could say anything, the commotion of cadets searching for their other team members came to a screeching halt. The group assembled and faced the direction of the proctors. Three of them signaled everyone to calm down as the rest of those standing behind them murmured. It took a moment for the Proctors to come forward and address what they were discussing. When they did, it shocked Anemone so that she wanted to groan.

"Attention, all CA2s!" Some spoke firmly. "The trials for today are on hold until further notice."

You could see restlessness roll through the corps of cadets. A giant clap of air sounded off before anyone could let a single complaint, springing everyone's focus on the sound. Everyone focused on commander Airelle, who was strutting between the crowd. He looked at the rows of Comrade-at-arms with every step, signaling them to stand down. When Airelle got to the front, his voice boomed into the cadets' chest. After everyone turned towards the stage in unison, he continued to talk.

"As much of you know, this is our first attempt at inter-Kingdom-based Accolade trials. Many of you expected this to be a kingdom-on-kingdom challenge, but it is not. Be grateful that all of you have a whole extra day to get acquainted with those you will be spending the next three days."

His glare scanned the crowd and landed in Anemone's direction.

"Her majesty's orders allowed this so that only a few die on this excursion."

Unlike the rest of her team members, none of them seemed afflicted. Her eyes scanned around, and she saw a few others mumbling under their breath, uttering the same word, "*Die.*" Spriggan warned her the trials were severe but were nothing compared to his youth. She knew that Commander Airelle was psyching everyone out.

"For those of you who are natives, go home tonight and tell your loved ones goodbye. For the rest of you. Pray to your fallen Celestials for their grace."

"Before you leave, know that we have shifted the testing zone from the Seelie Woods and the Mars ruins, not the Dogger Lowlands. Take this time to study the area's geography and prepare," the proctor added.

The mumbling of other participants stated a similar surprise. It was a larger area than they were expecting. Arielle turned his back, and everyone got dismissed. The circumstances were unexpected. Airelle's words and his eye shifting its focus in her direction was more than likely a coincidence. Anemone, on the other hand, felt it wasn't. Regardless of his tactics, it was too late for anyone to back out, especially since she wanted to keep her Grimoire. Most Comrade-at-arms had leased Grimoires until graduation. Once you did, you were allowed to register and maintain your Grimoire for personal use. Upon prompting to Knighthood, you can purchase one from Tir-noNog's inventory or make your own. However, if you decided the Arbor Magna was no longer for you, Grimoires were confiscated or returned to prevent the unrest of nonmilitary owning one. The circumstances of having some citizens able to use Ars more freely than others was a rising issue. If anyone found out she had been using an unregistered one, she was in absolute trouble, and so was Spriggan.

"Are ya getting cold feet?" Aronia placed her hand on Anemone.

She shuddered for a moment and bounced back. "No, it's just...."

"Well, if it's cool with everyone else, Imma disappear till tomorrow. That old guy's threats make me want to visit a brothel, and I can't go dying without my first nut." Rowan walked in the opposite direction.

"You are just the epitome of classy," Timber huffed as he followed behind.

Anemone called out to them. "Don't you think we should strategize and think about team dynamics"?

All the guys looked at each other, and Rowan spoke again. "In all fairness, the three of us have worked together before. I'm not going to lie; I kinda want to relax before we lose the opportunity to."

Timber stroked his chin. "I have to agree, though. Anemone has a point, and it wouldn't hurt to do so."

The two of them looked at Rubus to confirm.

"Don't make me the tie-breaker." I didn't volunteer to be the captain of this democracy."

Anemone raised her voice. "Wait, even if that is the case, it's 3-2 in favor of sticking together.

Aronia touched Anemone's shoulder. "I don't think they had us in mind."

"I'll pass," Said Rubus raising his hand. "No offense, but this is a three-day excursion, and the extra prep time sounds handy."

"How much prep time *alone* do you need? An hour wouldn't kill you," replied Anemone wither a raised voice.

"Sorry, but not this time, Wingless." Rubus walked off.

Anemone was getting riled up, and Aronia gabbed her before saying anything.

"No, it's fine, Nia. We aren't officially a team till we hit the turf."

Aronia looked at Anemone with absolute confusion. She knew how much she was looking forward to this moment. To see her so reserved about her displeasure was a shock. Timber bowed before he left, and the other two walked off in separate directions leaving Aronia and Anemone. Although Anemone thought discussing team synergy was excellent, she was glad they didn't want to go through it. The morning had already deflated her, and she was no longer up to the task. Now that they had left, she took it as a sign to worry about herself.

"Wow, this is the second time you've given up so easily. Did Ye speak to yer mum?" Aronia questioned.

Anemone turned away to hide her pouting face.

"Geez!" Her shoulder slumped. "She is not the only problem in my life."

"Yes, and I'm *apparently* engaged."

Aronia grabbed Anemone by both shoulders and pulled her face next to hers. "Explain!"

"It's Clausa, and it's political."

Aronia marched off, heading toward the direction of what Anemone assumed was the Tree of Dominion. Anemone quickly ran up to Aronia and grabbed her hand.

"I know what you're thinking, but—."

Aronia jerked her hand away from Anemone. "But nothing! Grow a backbone! Tell 'er how Ye feel!"

"It's more complicated than that!" Anemone folded her arms and averted her eyes away. "She's the queen and—."

Aronia shook her head as she interrupted Anemones to grab her shoulders.

"SHE'S YER MUM! THAT'S HER JOB TOO!"

"I'M JUST ONE PERSON!" Anemone slapped Aronia's arms off her.

"How I feel...doesn't matter...."

Aronia groaned, "Well, don't complain so much. If that's the route, Ye want ta take. Take it!"

"I'm sorry, Nia... Can't you let me complain in silence?"

"Fine. I already know Ye don't wanna go home now."

"No... Not really."

"Come on, Ninny. Let's unwind." Aronia grabbed Anemone's hand and pointed into the city as she smiled.

Anemones smiled back warily. "Ugh. That nickname is so tacky. Just stick to Nin like usual."

"Now, where's the fun in that? If yer goin' act like a child, I'll treat 'cha like one!" Aronia mocked with a smile that suddenly dropped. "Soon, I'll be the only one behind the walls."

"Y'know, it doesn't have to be like that."

Aronia rolled her eyes as she dragged Anemone away. Those were somber words, and trying to ignore their future with a walk through the city felt bittersweet. They had known each other since they were ten and were practically blood. Aronia was Anemone's only friend, only leaving each other's side for life's circumstances. The two of them had similar lives; Her mother, Florentina, was the head priestess for the Lauma tree, and her father was Prior of The Phloem Guard. Aronia also understood the burden of being the child of a revered figure. The only difference was that Aronia wouldn't let that rule over her life.

Although Anemone respected Aronia for it, there was a difference between being the daughter of a queen and the head priestess. Both were essential, but one did have some more weight to it. Instead of following the path of a priestess as her mother and father wanted, she wanted to join the Phloem Guard. Like Anemone, she heard war stories of time served in the Arbor Magna back when Spriggan and her father were younger. Baccata had served alongside Spriggan and also comfortably transferred into the Phloem Guard. He worked explicitly for interkingdom affairs, dealing with issues and communications between Tir-noNog and allies. Shadowing his work, Aronia found herself more interested in Baccata's duties than Florentina's. She didn't care much for anything outside Tir-noNog's walls unless mandatory. Anemone wished she could convince Aronia to follow her, but she was dead set on staying home. Tir-noNog was all that mattered to her, and serving her kingdom as police were her way of helping her home.

"Nia, I'm serious. Why—?"

"—Hey, Ninny." Aronia reached and held Anemone's hand. "About earlier this morning? You said you're seeing lights floating around other centers?

Anemone took a deep breath and laid her head on Aronia. "Yeah, but I'm not sure why."

"You still have those strange dreams? The ones where you're either walking down a long white corridor or slid across them? Are they connected?"

"I'm not sure... those were different." Anemone paused. "In those, I always heard strange voices and couldn't see anything but white walls and strange, white-clothed figures. This one was more real. A whole city and beings looked like Aos-Si, but their ears weren't pointy. It was so strange."

"How so?" Aronia stroked Anemone's hair away from her face.

"After I saw the flames or lights in the dream... the same ones appeared in some of the Aos-Si and Dragonkin here. But I don't know what they are."

"Did you talk to Spriggan?"

Anemone sat up and stared into the distance. "No, these flames were recent, yesterday recent."

Anemone knew Aronia was changing the subject, but she also knew Aronia cared about her strange dreams. Even when she had explained her other ones to Spriggan, he had no idea what she was saying. White halls weren't the only thing she saw in her dreams. She also saw a city filled to the brim with other beings walking around, wading through each other like merfolk swimming through the sea. Buildings of limestone and steel towered over anything constructed in Tir-noNog or Albion. The closest thing that resembled those buildings' sheer height was Albion's Grand Cathedrals, or maybe the Northern Towers the Dwarves built to keep an eye out for Dragons.

While her mind drifted into the clouds, the sight of a particular carriage caught her eye. It belonged to Titania and looked like it was leaving the city. Yet again, she was going for some unknown reason. Anemone planted her chin on her knees and scowled at the carriage. She remembered the last time she and Titania got in a fight; it was so long ago she had almost forgotten about it. Aronia was her strength; she knew having her next to her would keep her mind at ease. It was why Anemone wanted her to come along. That was when Anemone stood against her mother, thanks to Aronia.

"If it wasn't for that night, we might not have met."

...Two losses for a win

A s Aronia called out to Anemone, the blinding light of the sun's rays blurred the scenes of her running down a darkened alley. Her eyes locked on Aronia, with a wry smile snapping her fingers. Anemone was daydreaming and hadn't realized it. She recalled the moment they had met, but something felt off. It was almost like the memory had disappeared. As she tried to remember what had happened again, fog appeared over every moment of their interaction. The memory of her fight with her mother suddenly burned like flames to a paper. Aronia's lips moved as she tried to grab Anemone's attention, but there was no sound. Like a sudden snap of the fingers, Anemone began hearing again.

"Don't sit here gawking at that carriage! Go talk to her!"

Anemone could no longer see what she was trying to remember; her mind became hazy. She did not realize Aronia was telling her to go and talk to Titania. There was an entire lapse in their conversation, and she could not understand how. Her shoulders slumped, and she buried her face in her knees. Dealing with anything else was already too much. Anemone knew she couldn't put that off any further. They both knew that telling Titania she did not want to be married to someone she had only met twice in her life was reasonable. Telling Titania that Anemone wanted a world of adventure for herself, on the other hand, was out of the question. Titania's idea of unity through Anemone and Clausa's was sensible, but she didn't want it, even if it was for the sake of her people. After all her efforts to finally earn the right to participate in the trials, Anemone believed she deserved to reap the benefits. Beside Albion, the furthest thing she saw was the border right next to the Oryza Prairie.

"But it's for the sake of my people?" Anemone mumbled.

"Oh, please. Titania will live another two hundred years. I'm sure she can choose someone else. Or maybe even the Cabinet of Nine will."

"Nia, it's not that simple. The house of Anemone has held this kingdom together for five generations. Each one of them was vested in greatness. To be the only one who—."

Aronia looked at her and sighed heavily. "Is this for Ye or her?"

Anemone raised her head. "What do you mean?"

"Think about yourself for a change! Honestly, it's a grace and a curse with Ye. They'll all be fine without you."

"You just don't get it!" Anemone hopped to her feet.

"Get over yourself! They all believe that bloody superstition, and ever since that day, it's only gotten worst after you! Forget them!"

"I CAN'T!!!"

"YOU HAVE TO! OTHERWISE, YOU'LL LOSE THE CHANCE TO TALK TO HER LIKE ME!" Aronia pleaded.

"YOU AND FLORENTINA STILL HAVE TIME TOGETHER! WE DON'T!"

Anemone's words were hushed to a stop. Two things in that disagreement stuck out. The first was that last sentence, and the other was, "They'll be fine without you." It was the last thing she wanted to hear. Even if her people scorned and avoided her for not having wings or the Sylph's blessing because of superstition, they were her people. No matter what, Anemone still had to prove them wrong, not just for herself but for Titania. She couldn't focus on anything else.

But that last sentence cut even more profound than the other. The more Anemone thought about it, the more complex those words became. Anemone scratched her head as if she was on the verge of pulling out her hair. She had forgotten Aronia's situation.

"Did you really forget Nin? Seriously."

"There was so much on my mind I forgot about Heat Haze."

"Things like this make me glad I chose to stay here instead of going with you. Maybe Rubus is right."

"What did you say?"

Anemone shuddered at how his name popped up at a time like this. What could he possibly have to do with this? Was Aronia choosing him over her? When did they get so close, and why was she hiding their relationship?

"I guess you don't need me to," Anemone mumbled.

"What does that even mean, Nin? Fer faqs sake, I'm on yer side as well."

"Then why did you side with Rubus earlier? And why were you flustered when I asked about him the other night!? Why are you so bent on staying here when there's a whole world for us to see!?"

"FOR THE LAST TIME!" Aronia ended with a cough. "There is no world for US to see!" Another sudden cough erupted from Aronia. As she choked, more words escaped.

"You just want to run away from everything!"

A familiar voice called out and forced both of them to stop.

"Your Highness. Your mother would like to see you before she leaves."

"Yes... Hibernica," Anemone sighed.

"Oh, don't be like that. She's in a good mood today and surprisingly receptive. Both Spriggan and I have talked to her," Hibernica replied, throwing her thumb up.

"I'll believe it when I see it."

"Aro, I'll be taking Nin for a moment. Your convo will have to wait for later. Make sure you take more Salix bark tea. It will help for the time being."

"Don't worry, Sis. We're done anyway."

As Aronia walked away, Anemone clenched her arm. Anemone quickly walked past Hibernica and didn't look back at Aronia. What she heard from her made Anemone shudder as the words repeated in her mind. Anemone had forgotten about the Heat Haze slowly eating away at Aronia. All she could think of was how much time she saw

Aronia and Florentina spend together. Every time Anemone thought about how little Titania stayed around, the guilt only swelled. She shook her head, trying to ignore what she heard. It was hard to believe Aronia would say that. Anemone wanted to face the world head-on, not run away. The idea of her life revolving around Tir-noNog bounced between pride and disgust, but her duty came first.

Regardless of Aronia's words, she knew they would split paths irrespectively. Unlike Anemone, who wanted to see the world, being a Phloem Guard was her main goal. Being an Anther was secondary. Whether she got out of her arrangement, Aronia was more interested in staying home and protecting Tir-noNog. Heat Haze would have made it hard for Aronia to travel either way but staying here only seemed like a waste, especially if she didn't have much time left. For her to think about her life without Aronia was a sad realization. Hibernia's hand reached out and grabbed Anemone.

"You can't force things, Nin. Everyone has their *own* path."

"You say that, but unlike her, we are on predestined paths."

"If that's how you *choose to* see it, so be it."

Anemone was always tired of Hibernica's riddle-like nature. Even though she was one of her mother's vassals, Hibernica had practically raised Anemone. Being Aronia's older sister, she had spent a lot of time around both Anemone and Aronia, cultivating their studies. No matter where you saw her, she kept her dark oak hair wrapped up and covered by ceremonial veils just like Florentina. She usually wore Tir-noNog traditional dresses that looked nearly impossible to wear without tripping. Just seeing her attire made Anemone feel uncomfortable. Hibernica being twelve years older with a far softer disposition, made her far more approachable than Titania.

Along with her beaming smile constantly forcing you to act your best, she was the embodiment of killing them with kindness. Anemone wished she held her head high like her, but she never understood her way of thinking. Hibernica always found a way to make a positive spin on life, which always eluded Anemone. Trying to put a positive spin on her fight with Aronia would be more than complex.

Ignoring their digressions, Anemone began to agree with both her and Aronia. Perhaps this time, she could finally tell Titania how she felt. She'd either speak her mind or stop complaining about their relationship. Taking a deep breath, she rose to her feet. As she dusted off her pants, Hibernica patted her back to pump her up before meeting with Titania. Suppose all else failed, Anemone could stuff her face with dinner tonight at their home. Hibernica would be cooking dinner, so she'd have an excellent meal to cheer her up no matter how bad the conversation was.

Every step down the hill became swifter than the winds. Her throat felt dryer than sand, and her heart throbbed as she got closer to the carriage. The beating blasted so loud she kept looking at Hibernica to see if they could hear her heart as she did. It felt like there wasn't enough time to prepare her words. Why was she afraid of Titania? Was it that she could count the number of times they talked to one another? Was it the fact she never saw her smile? Was it the lack of freedom she had growing up? It was as if the world was trying to rush her to her strife.

It was at least a five-minute walk from the hills that overlooked their home, yet it seemed only seconds had passed. When Anemone had arrived at an arm's reach away from the carriage, her head turned back. She thought her eyes had betrayed her, but they had not. Although she perceived sweat was filling her hands, there was no sweat. "It was just a simple talk with her mother. How bad could it be?" It rolled through her mind on repeat. Anemone placed her hands on Titania's prized Tiger beetles. She saw Titania sitting in the carriage wearing her usual leather-hide armor. It was one sown from a Gallu-Minotaur she had slain. The Dwarven steel vambrace that bound her arms was battered but well-polished, just like the boots. Titania's eyes were focused entirely on a memo giving no attention to Anemone or Hibernica standing in front. As Hibernica opened the door, signaling Anemone to step inside, Titania spoke swiftly.

"That won't be necessary, Hibernica. Ninlil."

"Yes, Mother!"

"I said we'd talk, but I have to speak to King Gentiana in person for urgency. Remember, after the trials. The teleport gates are down, so I'll be going by carriage. You'll be sent to Albion to acclimate. So be ready."

"Mother!" Anemone gripped her left arm. Titania stopped looking at the memo, and her eyes rolled to Anemone. "About the trials...."

Titania looked at her, and her face softened. "Don't worry. The trials will commence before my return. I had the Phloem Guard do a final sweep of the area. At your level, you'll be fine."

Hibernica placed her hands on Anemone's shoulder and gave them a light squeeze with a smile. "See, your Highness? You know your mother is bad with words, but she does care. You should visit the Lauma tree and pray she keeps her promise."

Anemone stood confused, wondering if that was a compliment. It almost sounded as if Titania was affirming her skills. Anemone had heard harsher judgment from Titania before, but something about this was gentle. It was the affirmation she had hoped for, the closest she ever thought she'd get. For years, she asked for more trust from Titania; maybe today was a sign it was coming. As Anemone dwelled on the situation, she realized she never had a complete thought. Trying to spin it as Hibernica would, she convinced herself that her mother's disposition was a step forward on her part, but next time she would say something. Anemone touched her face as she saw the carriage riding into the distance. She could feel a faint smile stretch across her face. Anemone's steps became light as she skipped toward the great Lauma tree. Lie or not, she was going to claim it as a victory.

"Mother!" Anemone gripped her left arm. Titania stopped looking at the memo, and her eyes rolled to Anemone. "About the trials..."

Titania looked at her, and her face softened. "Don't worry, the trials will commence before my return. I had the Phloem Guard do a final sweep of the area. At your level, you'll be fine."

Hibernica placed her hands on Anemone's shoulder and gave them a light squeeze with a smile on her face. "See, your Highness? You know your mother is bad with words, but she does care. You should visit the Lauma tree and pray she keeps her promise."

Anemone stood confused, wondering if that was a compliment. It almost sounded as if Titania was affirming her skills. Anemone had heard harsher judgment from Titania before, but something about this was gentle. It was the affirmation she had hoped for, the closest she ever thought she'd get. For years, she asked for more trust from Titania; maybe today was a sign it was coming. As Anemone dwelled on the situation, she realized she never had a complete thought. Trying to spin it as Hibernica would, she convinced herself that her mother's disposition was a step forward on her part, but next time she would say something. Anemone touched her face as she saw the carriage riding into the distance. She could feel a faint smile stretch across her face. Anemone's steps became light as she skipped toward the great Lauma tree. Lie or not, she was going to claim it as a victory.

...The time has come

It had been a while since her last prayer visit, and Hibernica was correct to suggest it. The Lauma tree was another place she went to get peace of mind or pray to the Celestial for good faith. Around this time, the leaves were loose enough to pluck or drop onto the floor. After being blessed, they would be given to the Seamstress to weave clothing or pages for Grimoires. For the longest time, Tir-noNog was the only kingdom to produce Grimoires. Almost no other place had material that channeled Od and The Lauma's bark and leaves. Although production quickly outrivaled Lumenopal expeditions, its only drawback was that the branches and bark were nearly uncuttable, thus limiting yearly material production. The priestesses had finished collecting the leaves and bark for the season.

Anemone always found it amazing that even though Aos-Si lost their bond to the Od, the Lauma tree remained connected. Its power was so great it became the primary source of Tir-noNog's Barrier. Every generation of Fae royalty bonded with the Lauma tree syncing their Flux with it. Just as her mother did, so did Queen Medb and her predecessor before her, Mab. Soon Anemone would do the same, or she thought she would. She stopped in her footsteps and pondered what her future was. Would she find her life in the arms of a stranger from a country she only knew on paper? Or carry the legacy of her ancestors?

She had no idea how to make Titania see her as an asset for Tir-noNog. After years of shoving her nose in books and joining the Academy, nothing changed. She wondered if Titania was close to her parents, Queen Mab and King Dagda. The thought of Titania ever feeling down on herself sounded impossible. Instead, she spread her fist and slid her hands across its trunk. Anemone raised her hands to smash them into a nearby tree. Her hands froze before hitting it and hovered over the tree for a second.

"Am I this useless?" She whimpered. "Is all of this to play second fiddle in another kingdom!?"

As Anemone sniveled, the sight of guards in the distance caught her attention. She hid as she saw them leading a group of families through the Grove.

"How many more of these families do we have left?" She heard one of them. "The season is almost over."

"Don't know, but we've had to make more of these trips since we've had more immigrants."

"Yet the results are the same. The Barrier is shrinking."

Anemone had forgotten that familial prayers for the Barrier were still going on. Due to the decreased population, The Council extended the prayer period into the fall season. It was a law that every household visited the Lauma tree and prayed for good faith. The Council organized each family or individual by alphabetical lottery and assigned an escort to the Great Lauma tree. The ritual allowed them to rest for the day, leaving them free of responsibility. Although the process kept many satisfied and the Barrier strong, very few could venture close to it and needed a chaperone. The moment she overheard a sudden shrieking, she remembered why. Three of the fifteen Aos-Si were unconscious and carried by family members or guards. She could overhear them yelping in terror, shouting strange things.

"Not bad. Only three were overtaken by the fog this time," one of the guards spoke to another.

"Guess that means Head Priestess Florentina won't be as busy today."

"With only twenty-five Aos-Si being cursed by the fog today, it's a blessing."

Another one called out, "Silence! Your words will affect the morale of the prayers for the Barrier!"

Anemone never understood how the fog covering the area around the Lauma tree cursed others. The priestesses claim it was an Ars to keep those of lousy faith out. Those with bad faith or malice are driven mad and lost to the fog. The fog forces their mind to disappear into the beyond, and some even cackle in madness. It was an old tale the elders' told children, and having seen it before, she gladly did her best to live an honest life.

Her life aside, she had also heard about the Barrier shrinking. The Fae population had dropped after the Lost Wars, and so did the Barrier's strength which had once surrounded the entirety of the Tir-noNog forest and now only encompassed the kingdom. Titania had hoped to allow other Aos-Si to enter Tir-noNog, and their offered prayers would help, but it didn't seem to do as much. The Barrier was their home's greatest defensive asset next to the fog spreading southbound. If it weren't for the warp gate, almost anyone not native to Tir-noNog's land would be unable to step inside the kingdom. Besides the natives, only those sworn in would be allowed.

Once the group disappeared, Anemone continued towards the Lauma tree. Besides priestesses and chaperone visits, no one else came here for a breather besides Anemone. As frightening as it was, she found the fog comforting. Occasionally, she would sneak back here with Aronia for privacy and avoid the world. Since Aronia was an honorary priestess of the Lauma tree, no one would worry about seeing them here. With Florentina as her mother, Aronia often did priestess duties when she wasn't training or in the Academy. Over time Anemone found herself sitting alone. She didn't know why but as of late, Aronia had stopped appearing here as often.

After ten minutes, she wandered through the fog surrounding the Lauma tree. As she arrived at the trunk of the Lauma tree, she sat on one of its sprawling roots. The tree towered into the sky and oversaw the entire forest. It was almost impossible to approach even if you saw it outside because of the illusionary Barrier. Her eyes looked at a stone wedged in front of the tree.

"In honor of the Cloud Huntress, Warrior of the Thunderous blade."

She recalled stories of invaders stuck forever wandering these foggy woods. Titania used to trap rival tribes back when Fae was still at odds with Elves. Titania had prayed for victory during that battle, and in the end, she was victorious. It earned her another epitaph of The Cloud Huntress. Anemone remembered how everyone had told her the Celestials only listened to those willing to change the world. Titania led the Fae to an age of peace, along with Spriggan, a non-native who had crossed paths with the *Timeless Witch*, who found his way here. Anemone wished she, too, had such a will. One so strong she could create a way for herself just like them, but her life changed to no avail. If the world slowed down or something grand happened, maybe she wouldn't have to marry herself to a future she didn't want. She turned to the Great Lauma tree and held her Grimoire tightly as she began to pray.

"Great Lauma tree, I pray to thee. Allow me to show you my mettle. My lineage is from heroes. Queen Mab and King Dagda fought off the Unseelie, and Titania stopped the invasion of the Gallu-Utukku with aid from other Fae and Dwarves! Is there no trial left for me!?"

Anemone placed her hand on the Lauma tree and gripped its bark with all her strength. She leaned her head into the tree and called out again. Some of her knew it was foolish to call out to the heavens. If there was ever an opportunity for her world to change, now was the best time. She was tired of being bound to a place she didn't belong. As she slid her hand across the rough surface of the tree, she began to hate herself. Titania had fought against her mother's wishes to grab destiny by the reigns, yet she stood, afraid. Stories of Spriggan's journey and Titania seemed out of her reach, but maybe it was for the better. Perhaps it was selfish of her to want more from the world during peaceful times. Sure, the Gallu-Utukku and Therianthropes constantly killed and ate every one, but she was safe behind the walls. Many of the cadets wanted to be Phloem guards and stay safe. Why did she hunger for more, and why couldn't she eliminate her desire? Was she foolish beyond belief?

"So much for glory...."

She sat at the tree's base, and her eyes began to irritate her again. When she wiped them, she saw streams of light flowing through the tree's roots. It was so overwhelming that she kept her eyes closed to bear the light. Even as her eye remained closed, it was like staring into the sun, and the colors still blazed through her closed eyes.

The sound of sudden rustling caught Anemone's attention. Her head shifted from left to right as her vision flickered between regular and the strange hue. When leaves from the Lauma tree fell from above with a tint of gold flames, her eye looked to the skyward tree. From above, she heard a voice call out.

"The tree with the strongest roots bears the greatest fruit."

Anemone jumped to her feet. "Who's there?"

The area remained silent, neither the crack of a branch nor the sound of flowing winds. Anemone kept her eyes closed, but her hearing was sharp. There was no way someone could sneak up on her without her notice. Everyone in Tir-noNog knew that saying, so it could be anyone who was a priestess or guard. She knew the voice sounded unfamiliar to her, so she readied herself. It wasn't necessarily a deep voice, softer than Rubus' but a bit chipper than Aronia's.

"Sorry about that. I hope I didn't ruin your train of thought."

Their voice cracked as if they were trying to make themselves sound more mature.

"There's no way the tree is talking. Right?"

"No, I'm inside the tree." The voice cracked dryly.

When the wind started rustling the leaves, it made her realize someone was descending from the upper part of the tree. Thanks to the weird light emanating from that stranger's body, Anemone could still see him even with her eyes closed. Judging from their voice, she could tell they were male and not much older than her. If anything, she couldn't understand why they were projecting their voice in such a manner. As her vision returned to normal, Anemone saw him stuff his heels into the Lauma tree.

The motion of his skid was smoother than a cloth crossing freshly polished wood; It was almost silent. He hopped downward from branch to branch skillfully. Even Anemone found herself momentarily impressed. She almost thought he was as good as she was. However, instead of landing gracefully on his feet, his legs buckled beneath him. The force of his fall slammed his face into the ground. Anemone flinched as she gazed at his anticlimactic landing. Opening her eyes, she stared at the floor-planted stranger, hiding the urge to laugh at his failed landing. As he rose to his feet, he dusted himself off and picked up a mask that had fallen off.

"That was not how I planned that, but close enough."

Anemone placed her hand on her hips and scoffed, "This is sacred land... you don't just dig your heels into the Great Lauma tree."

"I can't say I saw a sign on the way in, but it's been a while since we've last met, hasn't it?"

Anemone folded her arms and shook her head since she had no idea what he was talking about or who he was. Although the fog was thick, she could see he had dark hair resembling the shaggy loose wool of a Big-horned Ovis. It was wide enough to cover his eyes, and she knew Dwarves would have sheered it for their clothes. When he whipped his face, she noticed the peculiar eye patch over the right side of his face. It almost resembled Spriggan's, with sigils scribed across the lower and upper part of the thick band that crossed his face, and it even had a Lumenopal shard hanging from it.

Once the fog cleared, she could see his face somewhat more transparent. The tattered navy-colored jacket mirrored the worn demeanor of his slumped shoulders. It was hard for her to assess the situation. He had to have been a resident born in Tir-noNog if he was this close to the tree, but no one beside her and Aronia ventured here by themselves. Seeing as he wasn't being driven mad by the fog, she assumed he couldn't be a threat either.

"I don't know who you are... Are you here for prayer?" Anemone stepped closer.

"Prayer? No, I was just reading this book I stole—" His words suddenly stopped. "—borrowed."

Anemone's smile turned severe as she drew her knife.

"If that's stolen property and you're trespassing. I'll be taking you in."

Without hesitation, she ran up to him with the blunt side of her sword breaker to strike the stranger. Her blade reached for his neck, but he knocked her arm away as he stepped to the side, throwing her off balance. Quickly Anemone took that momentum and raised her left leg to kick him in the face with the back of her heel. He responded just as swiftly by leaning back to dodge the blow. Leaning too far, he stumbled backward and placed his mask back on. Anemone entered into a squat to charge at him, and he fell into a half-bridge, raising his legs into the air to flip onto his feet. His kicks forced Anemone to stop in her tracks. Both of them stood there with their eyes locked on each other. Now that she was closer, she saw his Fog blot mask. She assumed he was no threat since he didn't land such a simple drop, but his swift reactions said otherwise. This time she wasn't going to take a chance.

The sigils on Anemone's arms glowed from under her sleeves, catching the stranger's attention. Her arms bulked as her muscle density increased to boost her strength.

"Arcane-Mono: 1st Tier: Gladius-(Arms)!"

With a flurry of slashes, she reached for vital areas around his chest to see his reactions. Only a few of her cuts came close to nicking his dark blue coat. Easily he parried every strike by hitting her wrist. As he caught her blades and tried to push her back, she let go of her knives and struck him in the jaw with her fist, stunning him. She then reached her hand behind his head and brought his face down as she raised her knee. She endured an impact, but her knee tingled like it had hit metal. Instead of flinching, she raised her knee again, but this time, she did it past his face, stomped her boot into his back, and launched herself into the air.

"Grimoire-Ars: Acquire inventory: Sword and shield-(Page 2)."

As he fell over, she came down, aiming her blade at him for a fatal blow, but his body glowed so bright it forced her eyes closed.

"Gold flames!? Why do you have those?" She called out.

Her blade pierced the earth below. When her eye reopened, she saw him sitting with a white flag raised and waved.

"I surrender."

She raised her shield and pointed her sword at his face. "I don't believe you for a second."

"Look, I know this is suspicious, but I'm looking for someone." He paused, raising the book. "I got side-tracked by this."

Her gaze locked on the book she had never seen before. It had the family crest and the phrase "Lost History."

"Where did you get that book?"

"This?" He pointed the flag at it. "I found it in one of those Tree buildings near here."

Anemone tried to think of what building was close by with books. The area where the priestess gathered was a hollowed-out tree, not a building. If anything, there were mainly scrolls and not books. It was a safety precaution to keep the secrets of crafting Grimoire as an oral tradition. Her eyes widened as she realized the only other place he could mean.

"You snuck into the Cabinet of Nine!?"

"I didn't sneak!!! I walked right in." He pumped his chest.

"Impossible! There are guards near the Grove, not to mention the priestesses!"

"Hey, it's not my fault they can't see Adnero-based Ars."

"Ad where-o based, Ars? What is that, and does it have to do with those strange lights?"

He sat there in dismay. "Weird lights? You can see Adnero?"

Anemone lowered her sword but kept her shield raised. Spriggan knew nothing of colored lights, so how could this stranger only a tenth his age understand? He could be lying and using some Phantasy Ars. Either way, she would get as much information from him as possible.

"Yes, I can. Now hurry up and explain yourself!"

"Jeez, you're aggressive. You act like I'm a criminal or something."

Anemone pointed her short sword at him again. "You stole a book, and I asked you a question!"

He tossed the book into the air with the slightest bit of movement. Anemone's eyes locked onto the text as it ascended. When her eyes dropped down from the book, he was gone without a trace. All she heard was his voice receding into the distance.

"Sorry, but I have somewhere else to be."

"Seriously!?" She called out. Quickly she dropped her sword and reached for the falling book. "That dolt should have been more careful about this."

The pace of their conversation left Anemone more confused than she wanted to be. When Anemone opened the book, she saw the words were in a non-Fae language. Upon inspection, its letters looked similar to Albionian Elvish but were different. As she raised the book more, a tiny pamphlet on how to fly with wings fell out. With her mind in turmoil, she didn't have the energy to translate it or continue to care.

"Grimoire-Ars: Inserta Inventory: Sword and shield-(Page 2) Lost Historia-(Pg 20)."

In a flash, the book and her weapons flew into the pages of her Grimoire. Suddenly she heard a soft ringing in the distance. At first, she thought nothing of it, but soon it became erratic. Her heart dropped because that wasn't the sound of any bell ringing. Those bells only rang when something that could threaten Spriggan or her was nearby. The Furin Bells warned the user that something was nearby they could or couldn't handle. Spriggan planned to use it to help Anemone gauge her foes for simple observation. Now it was warning her of something somewhere between her and his strength. She didn't know if she was ready.

...Night raid

The wind was ferocious as Anemone jetted back towards the city. When she looked at the sky, she could see the Barrier flickering. Tir-noNog was under attack, and it was something big by its looks. Hopefully, Spriggan returned from his patrol to handle the situation in Titania's stead. Once Anemone made it back into the city, herds of Aos-Si fled toward the safe zones. One of them rushed up to her in a panic. In the distance, she saw a priestess guiding everyone to safety.

"Your highness, the southern part of the Barrier broke. The 3rd District is under attack by Gallu!"

Suddenly the sensation of iron weights mounting her legs in place began. Her breath grew shallow as her body heated up. The alarm that went off in her mind was east, yet the attack was in the south. How was that possible? Was it a coordinated attack? Gallu often hunted individually, but coordination between two separate groups was unbelievable. She had never heard such a thing in her few years at the Academy. Not to mention Spriggan never mentioned that either. Their lack of peak intelligence gave everyone the advantage, but what had changed? Her mind recalled the Therianthropes that led that caravan from yesterday. They had already been dealt with before, but there was a chance another group made its way to Tir-noNog.

Whether she should head south or east bounced through her mind. If she went east, she would be alone. Anemone knew she wasn't ready, but the fear of no one else stopping what it was motivated her to make a move. The image of that Elf popped into her mind again. As her heart prepared to leap out of her chest, she thought of Spriggan. He would be on the front lines defending the wall if he were here. There was no reason for her to hesitate. Only they knew where he had set up the Furin Bells, and she had no choice if he was too busy.

"I have to head to the eastern side of the forest! Use a whisper to tell Spriggan and send any extra Commander rank troops there!"

Anemone darted off without hearing the priestess. Even if she didn't have a chance, she could at least distract it until more support arrived. She might even prove viable in her mother's eyes if she survived. Judging by the sound of the bell, it was a long shot. Wading through the crowd was like tree-hopping in the Tir-noNog woods on its windiest day. Every step she took had a body crash into her. The screaming masses of Aos-Si, who rushed past Anemone, drowned out her thoughts.

They almost knocked her off her feet as it got harder to move straight through the crowd. Instead of continuing on the ground, Anemone jumped from everyone and hopped onto a nearby Vulcan Lumenopal streetlight to get a better path forward. From the corner of her eye, she could see a few CA2s guiding the crowd of Aos-Si fleeing toward shelters. It wasn't long before she saw Timber and Rubus on the sidelines doing the same. Although she noticed them, she wasn't sure how willing they would help. In any case, she had to hurry.

Hopping across a few more, the sight of a child stuck in an alley caught her eyes. The look of him trying to cross the Aos-Si River almost caused her to lose her balance. She saw another one huddled up in an alleyway directly across from him as she regained her footing. Putting two and two together, she let out a sigh.

"I swear, it's always children!" she thought. "I should help."

A thought of whether her helping them was worth it crept into her mind. She genuinely thought their parents would only shrink, knowing she helped. Either way, she hopped down. She stood next to the young Elf to ask him if he needed help getting across. He shook his head and wiped his face. She grabbed him in one arm, leaped back onto a streetlight, and then across to another, landing right into the other alley. The young Elf shook his head and thanked her.

"Are you two okay? Where are your parents?" Anemone asked.

The younger one nodded while, the older one fought back the tears to cry. "B'ma a miner, we haven't seen her in months, but A'ma was running with us."

"She told me not to let go, but my leg hurt, and I—" the older one sniffled.

Anemone rubbed his head to stop his tears. "Don't worry, we'll find her! No need for those tears. You're proud, TirNog Fae! Save those for joy."

They smiled at her, and she grabbed them, telling them to hold on. Even with their added weight, picking them up and hopping from the alley to the top of the tailor shop nearby was easy. Their scared faces faded, switching to excited glee as the wind brushed past their faces and the force of gravity tugged at their legs. When she landed, they tugged at her sleeve to do it again—their smiles made her laugh.

"Weren't you two scared a second ago? What does your mother look like? What was she wearing?"

As she held their hands, the children described their mother as wearing a red shirt and having purple hair. After a dozen red shirts ran by, Anemone was beginning to think it was better to take them to one of the shelters and have someone watch over them until the attack finished. However, it was quite the task in a crowd of wildly-haired colored Aos-Si running to safety.

A sudden flash of fire rising into the air caught her eye, and she saw Rubus standing next to a Succubus when she turned her head. The two children jumped in glee as they saw her, and Anemone grabbed them and hopped down.

"A'ma," they both cried.

"My babies!! May Albrecht bless you, cadets."

Her face froze when she realized it was Anemone. Her mouth closed, and she nodded as she grabbed her young Aos-Si into her arms and ran off.

Anemone's voice fell from a yell to a whimper. "No thanks necessary...Just hurry to a bunker."

"You're a real Paragon, Wingless." Rubus raised his fist to fist-bump her.

Anemone folded her arms. "So are you. Why are you here?"

He shrugged his shoulders. "A knight passed the mom onto me since he was heading east. There's another horde on the eastern side, but I guess that's where you're heading?" He tucked his hands into his pockets.

Anemone let out a sigh of relief. "Yeah, it was, but I have less to worry about now."

"So that is what you were after? A chance to slay something? I never figured you for the hunting type."

"Shut it, and I don't—" The bells' echoing sound rang again, but even louder. "Why is it ringing again?

"Ringing?"

The sound of the "Furin Bells" became irritatingly nonstop. The bell had barely rung so loudly before. Even with those knights going without Spriggan, Anemone dripped with unease. As sweat dripped from her brow, she clenched her fist, and before she knew it, she proceeded anyway. She hopped across the rooftops and continued towards the eastern forest. Although she was afraid, something was guiding her forward.

"Wingless, you damn Treehopper! Wait up!" Rubus called out as Anemone fled.

...First Blood, First Sight

Only twenty flights away, she began to feel the presence of whatever had the bells so hysterical. It didn't take her long to get close. Her mind imagined it would be anything from a Mimic to Lycanthropes, judging by the moon's height. The lunar cycles often allowed one to predict whatever might be possessed by the curse of the *Gallu*-Utukku. With full moons and new moons having the strongest creatures as threats, many Aos-Si avoided the night on those days. When she arrived, she saw no soldiers or any monsters. Only a robed individual was present. Judging from their stature, they were not much taller or more muscular than her. But the robe made it hard for her to tell what they were. She stayed above and observed them, ensuring they couldn't see her.

They continued forward with a steady pace, whistling as they swayed their head to the beat of their steps. The air was heavy, yet there wasn't a sense of urgency in their movements. Anemone thought it was rotten luck that something this strong would appear when Titania or Spriggan wasn't here. The fact they were heading in the direction of Tir-noNog was no coincidence. She drew her blades, ready to attack just in case. A rustling sound from behind her caught her attention, and she instinctively tossed her knife in that direction. A loud thud sounded as the blade pierced the bark of the tree.

"Are you mad?!" Rubus yelled.

Anemone's eyes widened, and she huffed, "I told you to stay back!"

"No, you didn't. The moon is high. Also, don't be stupid. Leaving you alone is—."

Anemone raised her finger to her mouth, and Rubus quickly silenced himself. He pulled her knife from the tree and hopped next to her. Instantly her head swiveled left to right.

"They're gone."

"Who?"

"The robed individual."

"What are you—?"

Without a beat, a gust of air burst past Anemone, and as her eyes squinted, all she could see was glowing yellow sigils streaming past her. Something sent Rubus flying to the ground when she turned around, and its eyes were blazing at her. Before she could think, the glowing creature launched itself at her. Rings on her legs glowed as she dashed out of the canopy.

"*Sigil* cast: Kinesthetic."

Anemone quickly stuck her knife into the tree to slow her descent and flung herself behind some branches. She was glad she had scribed the sigils and glyphs on her legs to quick cast. Even with the spell, the pain from the scars on her arms was still present. A burning sensation appeared in her arm, but the glowing beast occupied her focus. The sheer force of its lunge threw her jump off as she tumbled into the air.

The creature followed suit, and she found herself weaving in and out of the tree's components. As she kept her eyes on it, she could see the figure. Their legs were stubby, with long, dangling, meaty arms and fangs that looked like they could tear armor. As it roared again, its figures became more pronounced by the outlines of its *sigil*s. From the light of the *sigil*s and moonlight peeking through the upper canopy, she saw its dark gray fur; it was a Lycanthrope possessed by a *Gallu*-Utukku. Seeing as it could only toss itself full power in one direction, she knew the *Gallu* controlling it was young. Had the *Gallu* adapted to the new body more, it would have killed her. Anemone kept out, maneuvering it hoping to tire it out.

The battle had become a match of deadly tag, but she was handling herself just fine. The only question was, how long would she have to do so? After five minutes of bouncing around, she sensed her legs were at their limit. She focused on how fast it was moving the whole time she jumped. Slowly she was getting a grasp of its movements. Anemone headed for the ground and looked upward. The *Gallu*-Lycan followed her as she hoped. She cast a Gladius-Ars and powered her arms with all her strength, flying towards the *Gallu*-Lycan. Before she reached it, its body combusted into flames. As it burned, it yelped furiously, and Anemone pierced its chest without hesitation. The *Gallu* grabbed onto Anemone, and they fell to the ground.

It was so hot the heat of the flames burned over her body. Anemone didn't let the heat get to her, and she twisted her knife deeper. It gnarled and furiously gnawed at her face. Like the clanking of metal, the snaps of its teeth sent shivers down her spine. Even with its body engulfed in flames, it didn't bother to stop aiming for her throat.

"If only these arms of mine could do more!" She thought.

Anemone hated how weak her arms were and cursed that accident. If it hadn't happened, maybe they would be at full power. She couldn't believe how nasty this thing was, and if it wasn't so focused on chewing her face-off, it might have ended her with one swing of its arm. Far off, she heard someone cast a spell.

"Sylph-Mono: 2nd Tier: Aer Gae-(Lycanthrope)!"

A spear-like air strike stabbed through the left side of its face and arm, forcing the creature to rise and howl in pain. Blood flowed from the cavities, and her knife bored deeper into its chest, splashing all over her face and torso, nearly blinding her. She quickly rolled over and dashed away.

"Grimoire-Ars: Inventory Acquire: Bow-(Pg 12). Vulcan arrow-(Pg 13)."

Her Grimoire flashed, and a bow appeared in her arms and a single, red-tipped arrow. As she turned and leaped upward, she saw the beast rumbling towards her with three more spears of pressurized air stabbed into its body. The moment she let loose the arrow, embers from it mixed with the swirling wind and erupted. The *Gallu*-Lycan roared as it tried to roll out the flames around it. Once its eyes set on her again, she drew another arrow and pulled a page from her Grimoire.

"Grimoire-Ars: Inventory Release: 10x-Vulcan Arrows-(Pg 13)!"

Anemone let the arrow loose with a page tied to the needle. A barrage of ten Vulcan arrows appeared next to that single flying arrow, shooting straight for the *Gallu*. Its body got showered by almost every arrowhead and exploded as it pierced its eyes, chest, and legs. The creature hardly relented, only stumbling and rolling back to its feet. Anemone landed on the ground, ready to swing her bow into the face of the rabid monster. She heard another Sylph spell cast in the distance. A storm appeared from under the *Gallu* and sent it flying. Its movement slowed as its body spun, rising high into the sky. Rubus emerged from behind some shrubs calling out another spell.

"Fall! Sylph-Mono: 1St Tier: Storm Eye-(Lycanthrope)"

A pillar of compressed air slammed into the *Gallu*, spiraling into the ground. Its body let out one last cry before the light in its eyes faded. Anemone could see black flames appear across its body. She leaned on the tree behind her, and her body curled into a ball as her arms shook violently. Even though she had long stopped fighting the *Gallu*, the weight of its body pulsed through her arms. Her bow was still firmly grasped in her hands, and even when she tried to let it go, they wouldn't listen. She gazed at her arm to check the burning sensation from earlier. The cut she received earlier had slightly stung from the heated grasp of the *Gallu*. It was pretty deep, but she could tell there were no lacerations.

"Calm down... you're still alive," she whimpered.

The phrase repeated in her head over a dozen times, but it didn't help as her mind replayed the sight of its long rotten, broken fangs clamping at her face. The smell of decaying flesh from its breath burned itself in her nostrils. Tears leaked from her eyes no matter how hard she fought them. Suddenly her entire body was in pain, and she didn't know what to do.

"Not too bad, Wingless."

She heard Rubus's voice shoot from behind the tree. Anemone wiped her tears as she gritted her teeth from the pain of minor burns. Doing her best to fake strength, she spoke with a lackadaisical attitude.

"What did you expect?"

"I suppose you're right. I shouldn't expect less from the daughter of savior Fae Titania."

"Thanks for the barbecue." She raised her arm with a spiteful tone.

"Tyndre was the quickest long rage Ars I had," He sighed. "I'll be more careful next time."

She was taken aback by how considerate Rubus was, as he always projected a standoffish-like character. After wiping her face one last time, she stood up from behind the tree and faced him.

"Rubus, it's the dead of night, and we just fought monsters. Why do you still have your eyes covered?"

He pointed at her face. "Unlike you, I don't want people to see my eye at times like this."

She turned to the side to avoid eye contact. "So that you know, I wasn't crying... blood got in my eyes."

"Crying? No, I meant-"

The sound of clapping hands quickly caught their attention, and a sudden pressure began to choke Anemone again. This time the force had brought her to her knees. From the corner of her eye, she could see Rubus's hands clenching in the air as they were ready to grab something.

"Well, that's quite an achievement Ninlil." The hooded figure appeared from the shadows of the forest. "You didn't lose an arm this time," they continued with applause.

"So, *you* tripped the Furin!" she called out.

"You thought that pathetic excuse of a creature did that!? I'm offended!" Their applause stopped.

A sudden violent roar of air passed Anemone and cut her hair loose, blinding her eyes. Her head turned and landed on Rubus, who drew his blade as the wind roared around it.

"Where is Chimera!!?"

The robed figure stroked their face as they tilted their head

"And you are?"

After a few more strokes of their chin, as if they were in a moment of deep thought, they planted their clenched fist into the palm of their hand.

"Well, shit... if it isn't Cynareae's bastard gene pool. I can't believe you became a Silver Soldier. That Dökkálfar blood ain't no joke."

"*Cynareae?*" Anemone thought. "*Isn't that the deceased king of Albion?*"

"Sylph-Elemancy!"

Rubus quickly lunged towards them with a raging battle cry and disappeared in a flash. Before Anemone's eyes could register his movement, Rubus reappeared in front of the robed individual. His voice howled as his sword pierced their chest and drilled violently with a whirlwind raging behind Rubus. Silence loomed over the area right as his presence vaporized.

"Ahhhhhh!!!" the Robed individual's voice cracked with a mocking cough. "Oh no! The pain."

Rubus's eyes widened as the words left his mouth with a whimper, "You can't be serious?"

The strike only blew their hood off and revealed a plain mask with a fog-shaped symbol. It was too dark to see the color of their tied-back hair, but Anemone could tell that mask was familiar. It was similar to the one she had seen earlier near the Lauma tree. There was no way it wasn't that stranger from before.

"I'm glad you noticed I'm not," they taunted as their arm reached out and clutched Rubus's throat. "Take a load off, kiddo."

The same sigils that appeared on Anemone's legs as she cast Gladius Ars shined through the sleeves of his robe. The individual spun around twice before sending Rubus flying at Anemone. Without enough time to react, she suddenly felt her chest compressing from the full force of Rubus slamming into her. If it wasn't for the tree's trunk, they might have flown into the darkness of the night. As her back collided with the tree, her mind went blank, forcing her body to gasp for air. Both of them coughed up blood as they leaned over in pain. Anemone could hardly keep her eyes open as the robed individual walked forward. The ground started to rumble as Anemone began to lose consciousness.

As her eyes scanned the area, the scenery became colorless, and it was almost hard to decipher the outline of all the trees around them. A white Grimoire rose from behind them and shined a light that beamed into her eyes. Soon the color of the world started to return as the stranger's body was shrouded in those black flames from her dream.

"Don't worry. Nin, I don't need to kill you yet."

She saw another Gallu-possessed creature blasting through the forest as her eyes closed. It was oversized, with crystal-like shards protruding from its thick brown fur, but she couldn't decipher what it was from her blurry vision. Its voice hollered as it tossed trees aside like mere twigs. Anemone slammed her arms into the ground to hold her body over an unconscious Rubus. Her vision blurred more, going in and out, and as her eyes blinked, they disappeared. Like magic, the *Gallu* replaced his body as if he wasn't there.

"I can't die just yet...."

...Another fright under a turbulent night

The sound of wooden wheels creaking rocked Anemone's mind as her vision slowly returned. Her eyes blinked, and a darkened wood ceiling blocked the skyline. She hopped up in place and reached for her knives. Without feeling them on her hips, her eyes scoped the surrounding area. She noticed she was inside a carriage and turned her head to see Rubus' body.

"You're just ready to stab something, aren't ya?"

"A vulnerable warrior is a dead one," Anemone groaned. "What happened?"

"Muspel, if I know, I also got knocked unconscious."

Rubus had a disappointed look on his face, and Anemone was confused. She had honestly thought she should have died, but she didn't. A sense of relief and air filling her lungs made her feel great that she was still alive. Her arms still ached from before, but it was far more bearable. Her eyes widened as she turned to the front of the carriage.

"SPRIGGAN!!!"

"Awake at last, Sprout?"

Her body slumped as she slid down the side of the carriage to the floor. She was embarrassed at her performance. She should have handled a single *Gallu*, and although she didn't want to admit it, Rubus was a significant help. If he hadn't been there, she might have died. After all those years of training with Spriggan, she still ended up being saved by someone else.

"Relax, Sprout, a *Gallu*-Fauna of that size would have caught anyone off guard. With that many numbers, be grateful you got away with your life."

"That many?"

"The two of you were able to defeat three of them, and that's pretty good for your ages," Spriggan continued.

Anemone had no idea what he was saying. She had only fought one with Rubus's help, and there was no way they had defeated more of them. When she looked at Rubus, he shrugged his shoulders.

"After I got knocked down, two more *Gallu*-Lycans came after me. I had to deal with them before returning to help you."

She couldn't believe that Rubus could handle two of them independently. Meanwhile, she could hardly hand one by herself. Although she knew Spriggan was right, she still hated how it was a struggle to hold off a juvenile *Gallu*. If she had struggled that much now, how could she hope to defeat one?

"You were lucky Rubus followed after you. You were brave for trying, but you should have waited."

Anemone jumped up. "You told him?!"

"Really? You're mad I told him you tried to do your job?"

"No, it—"

"—Was foolish of her to have even attempted to do that on her own," Spriggan exhaled.

She didn't want to hear it. Even if it was true, knowing that even Spriggan believed she wasn't enough on her own hurt her pride. Initially, she had only wanted to observe what was activating the Furin, but one thing led to another. She wouldn't have struggled so much if she had only had control over an Elemental Ars like Rubus. If she had more power, she wouldn't have even needed him. She clenched her fist and placed her forehead into it. Rubus's face grew a puzzled look across it.

"Why, she's Titania's daughter? She's had first blood before." He paused and squinted. "Hasn't she?"

Both Spriggan and Anemone stayed silent. She could feel the judgment in his eyes staring her down. They had planned to take her into the deeper part of the woods to hunt down Vespula, but it never happened. Anemone never got the opportunity to hunt something. Spriggan and Titania were too busy, and she didn't make a big deal about it. The only problem was it was *absolutely* a significant expectation from everyone in the Arbor Magna.

Rubus raised his brows. "You're kidding, that *Gallu* was her first kill?!" He leaned back and nodded. "Well, shit."

The silence on the way back was excruciating to Anemone, and it stayed until they arrived near Tir-noNog's gates. She wanted to ask about the robed individual that disappeared and how Spriggan defeated that oversized *Gallu*. Sadly, her failure and thoughts about Rubus's opinion kept her mouth shut. Spriggan solved everything while she was knocked unconscious. All she wanted to do was go home and get some rest. After all, her trials were on hiatus until further notice. She was better off focusing on something she could handle. Rubus hopped out of the carriage without looking at Anemone.

"He thinks I'm weak... Doesn't he?"

Spriggan responded in an interested tone, "I'm surprised you care."

"I don't, but...." Anemone dropped her head to her knees. "He's on my team."

Spriggan fought to hold back his laughter. "Is that so?"

"DON'T LAUGH! It's embarrassing! The world has it out for me!"

Her knees muffled the cries of her voice. After internally screaming her head off for a moment longer, she peered one of her eyes out and stared at Spriggan's back.

"You're disappointed too... Aren't you?"

He held his breath and stared into the sky as if looking to the heavens for the right words.

"Sprout, you could have died... You could have and should have used the Whisper-Ars I left in your Grimoire to tell *any* soldier near you. It was a horde of fifteen, and those four slipped by."

Anemone raised her head. "I told a priestess, but I didn't know you left a "Whisper" in the Grimoire, and I wasn't sure if you had come back." She paused.

"I just wanted to be useful. You've done much to hone my skill, and I wanted to show you it wasn't for nothing. I could have just continued to observe, but one thing led to another. I'm sorry."

"I'm just glad you're alive. What would your mother have said?" He exhaled.

"Forget, mother! It's not like anything I've done ever mattered to her."

"That's not true. Titania delayed the trials for you."

Anemone didn't want to believe her mother could be so considerate. The Titania she knew was cold and distrusting. No matter what Anemone did, she could never amount to anything.

"She could at least act like it. She didn't have to leave so soon—." Spriggan interrupted Anemone.

"Titania left again? Did she say why?"

"Muspell, If I know. She's like a damn wall! Except a wall will support you when you lean on it."

The smell of flowers suddenly caught Anemone's attention. Her thoughts were so focused on her failure that she failed to realize someone was sitting next to Spriggan. The whole time they were silent and perfectly still. They never bothered to turn around, so she couldn't see their faces. She knew they weren't the robed individual from earlier, judging from their stature. Before she could ask who they were and what else had happened, Spriggan stopped the carriage in the middle of the road.

"I need you to spend the evening at Baccata's."

"Nia's house? Sure, but why?"

"Don't worry about it. Clausa will be at the Tree of Dominion, and I know you'd rather avoid him after your day."

Anemone hesitated before she disagreed, but he was right. She stood up and hopped out of the carriage. When she got out, she turned to Spriggan since she still wanted to talk to him more. However, the sudden sight of her gear falling out of the air caught her eye as she fumbled to grab everything. When she looked up again, the carriage was riding off with Spriggan, who had a smile as he waved.

"You'll be fine," he said, pointing at his left eye. "I'd bet my good eye on you pulling through."

Even though Anemone experienced some reassurance, something felt off, as if life was bouncing her around from moment to moment. It wasn't unusual, but she hoped to get more off her chest. Still being alive felt like a consolation prize. The more she thought about it, the less she wanted to remember it. Her eyes stared at the carriage as it continued down the road. As the chill rolled down her spine, she could no longer tell if the cold winter winds were coming or something else. When she turned to her side, her boot stepped on shattered glass. The somewhat dry puddle surrounding it had an oozing reddish tint. Looking up, the sight of the Fourth District was full of damaged buildings, and the rubble-filled streets made her body shudder. She knew it was a puddle of somewhat singed blood when she gazed at her feet again. Following its trail, she noticed it leaked from a nearby crushed home.

Anemone rubbed her shoulders as she turned left and walked down the road seeing fragments of Cinnabar Lumenopal shards that once-lit light posts scattered near destroyed dwellings. With every step, the sound of glass squeaked and crushed beneath her boots. The streets were brimming with roasted wood, earth, and blood. The only thing that lit the streets now were a few surviving Evermoss plants on the side of the road.

The remains of the broken home reminded her of what she should be fighting to protect. Unlike the others here, she had survived her first encounter. The sight of those fangs popped into her head, and she could remember the smell of rotten flesh. She didn't know if it was from the dead bodies under the rubble or her memories. As much as she tried to be intense, fear still crept up from the back of her mind. The circumstances were far more jarring than the stories she heard. Phloem Guards and medics ran around headless, tending to the wounded. Anemone did her best to keep her eyes forward, avoiding eye contact with anyone around her. Judging from the lack of runic seals on the standing buildings, she knew it was a district for those without Ars. Od-less always got the short end of the stick, even in the well-protected Tir-noNog. A Gallu or Unseelie wouldn't often sneak inside or break through the city's barrier. But when they did, the Od-less only had prayers and luck.

As Anemone arrived at another crossroad, a patrol of Phloem Guards in the distance caught her focus. The CO talked to two other guards, and she could overhear them. They said the *Gallu* ate some of the Aos-Si in this district before anyone could help. Anemone could feel the weight of her arms grow heavy again. She took a deep breath and channeled Arcane Od to calm herself. Even then, she found it hard to stop her arms from shaking. When she crossed paths with the Patrol, the CO called out.

"Your highness, it's too late to be out now. Please return home. We just had an attack."

She turned to the CO and responded, "Don't worry, Commander, I'm headed there. I just—"

His eyes caught her Grimoire, and he interrupted her words.

"Ah! I see you have a Grimoire now. Soon you'll be ready to fight just like the Thunderous Titania!"

Anemone stumbled before she spoke, "... Of course! I have to do what I can to be just like her."

He nodded in affirmation. "That's the spirit! You don't need elemental Od to be as great as her. Just your will."

"Just her will," another guard hissed.

She always hated the platitudes she heard from everyone about her *will*. Everyone in the military knows Od-less doesn't get that respect and her royal blood kept her in better standing with older officials. When she was among her peers, it was a different story. From the cover of her eye, she could spot the other officers her age snickering.

"If you don't mind, your majesty, I'll need to verify it with the Lumen Index."

"Of course! We wouldn't want any Grimoires not connected to our Habakrem. That would be dangerous."

Sweat began to drop from Anemone's brow as the CO stuck his hand out. Inside his hand was a ring the size of a bracelet called The Lumen-Index. It had five Lumenopal shards, each corresponding to the type of Od channeling through the book. The first two were Cinnabar, the stone that burns red with Vulcan Od, and Saffron gleaming of earthy Oread. And the other three were the Cerulean cooling stone of Undine, Celadon, the stone of temperamental Sylph, and the Amethyst of mysterious Arcane. As she looked at the Lumen-Index, her heart was ready to hop out of her chest. It was the first time she would have her Grimoire scanned since she got it from Quarz. Anemone held her breath as the CO opened the front page of the Grimoire under the Lumen-Index ring. Its runic sigils glowed over the serial number written, matching the purple wavelength of the Amethyst Lumenopal.

"The Lumen-Index checks out, your highness. Be safe homebound."

Anemone let out a huff of air. *"I guess Spriggan already linked it to the Habakrem,"* she thought.

She didn't know when he had the time to set it up with Quarz, but she was glad it had already happened. It was proof that its Arcane energy flowed through it from Tir-noNog's rainbow-colored Habakrem. Every kingdom had one attached to it, and most either drew on its Od directly or channeled it into their Lumenopal shards or Grimoires. The primary way to recharge a Grimoire was through a

Habakrem since its fragments usually came from it. You could use a random Lumen-vent or Pylons found in the wild to restore them, but stones themselves were often temperamental. Sometimes they didn't work as well if you did so. If push came to shove, you would have to change the entire Lumenopal shard wedged into the book.

Staring at the ring again, she began fighting her body's urge to deflate. Fae of today considering Arcane-only users as Od-less always haunted her. Sure, she couldn't cast Elemental-Ars without conversion, but Saboteur and Synergist-Ars were just as valuable. Or that's what Spriggan taught her. Since Aos-Si began being born with less Elemental Od, everyone became hysterical. It didn't help that those who had only Arcane weren't as proficient with it, and she was the exception to that rule. Anemone could be as gifted as some older warriors by the Celestial's grace, but many were still elitist.

Being the daughter of The Thunderous Titania, who shot thunderbolts without a Grimoire, only compounded their pity. Anemone closed her eyes and reached for the book. When a rush of energy sparked her hand, she opened her eyes again and saw the light from the other shards. The CO closed her Grimoire and handed it back to her as if nothing had happened. Anemone took her Grimoire back and laced it to her hip as she walked off, shaking her head.

"If they didn't notice anything, my mind is playing tricks with me," she thought.

Before she continued her walk to Aronia's home, she overheard the two officers behind the CO being stern with someone else. Once Anemone noticed the blackened sclera and winged hips, it was easy to tell they were a Pixie. Because of the myth, Anemone already knew they would have their eyes on any Unseelie in the surrounding area. She stopped in her tracks and thought if she should say something. Of course, discriminatory actions were unacceptable, but the Phloem Guards looked out for each other.

Everyone was on edge with high tensions after the recent Gallu assault. The urge to say something boiled in her chest, but she didn't have the will to deal with the discussion. She had barely survived her first contact with a *Gallu* and had no more energy left. Every time she saw it, she endured her powerlessness. Even with her royalty status, she could stop it now, but not permanently. Why was everyone so set on finding a reason to fight each other? Why continue to dwell on the past? They had all heard the weight of war and its losses, and the Gallu-Utukku were always a treat. As she turned to say something, a powerful gust blew by. Before Anemone could utter a word, a loud crash sounded off.

"Oh, what now!?"

...Birth of their story

The sound of wind erupting blasted through the streets, cracking any leftover windows. Anemone covered her face and prepared for the worst. With the Lauma Tree peeking into the sky, strong winds occasionally came down into the city below and blew Aos-Si away. Many architects made windows reinforced to survive winds exceeding storms. The winds that just blew had to be a powerful Sylph-Ars. Her eyes scoured the area through the spaces between her fingers to see where it came from. Suddenly a large thud rumbled on the ground between her and the Phloem Guards. As a cloud of dust expanded, a body rose from them.

"Well, I wasn't expecting him to blow me away... figuratively and literally," a masked individual responded.

As their mask fell off and exposed a face, Anemone roared. "It's the mask from earlier!"

Her hands reached for her daggers as a gentle gust of air blew through the street. Soon after, a snide voice shouted.

"I'm going to need you to come with me, Denizen. Your kind is a rarity, and Grandfather would be pleased!" Acaulis landed from the sky.

The young male dusted himself off. "Y'know... you usually tell someone to come with you before you try to kill them. Unless you're into necrophilia, I won't judge."

Acaulis pointed his blade. "Your conversational skills are worse than mine. Even I must admit that was tasteless."

Acaulis eyes when straight to Anemone once he noticed her. He called out to her with his usual arrogant tone. "Quickly! Wingless Princess, capture him!"

The stranger turned to lock eyes with Anemone. As the two stared at each other for a second, a devilish smirk grew across his face. She flinched at his crudeness, and now that the fog was gone and there were no strange lights, his look was unmistakable. He had a patchy trim beard across his chin that matched the rugged look of his loose wooly black afro. His immature voice almost mirrored the shape of his round yet sharp face. It was the first time she had seen a Denizen, and she realized how similar they looked to Aos-Si. The only difference was the un-pointed ears and lack of vibrant skin color, much like herself. Before she could move, he vanished. His gray eye abruptly reappeared only a few inches away from her own.

"I guess we meet again, Lydia" he smirked as he raised his hand near her face. "Sorry, and thanks in advance."

"Who are you—"

Anemone blinked, and he placed his index finger on her forehead. Her body dropped, and as he caught her, he threw Anemone's seemingly lifeless body over his shoulders. It emblazed itself with a Gold Flame, and Anemone quickly recalled her dream of seeing streets filled with black flames.

"Don't worry. I'm only kidnapping you as leverage or a meat shield. Whichever works for you."

"UMMM, neither!" She yelled as she struggled to move, but her body didn't respond.

"Anybody moves, and the Princess gets it!" He prodded at her hips

Acaulis scoffed and summoned spears of wind next to his body. "Aer— !"

Anemone saw the CO grab Acaulis by his shoulders to stop him from launching his spell. Acaulis leered at the officer as he tried to stop him. Anemone's eyes widened as she realized Acaulis had no intention of yielding. She understood he was arrogant, but Aer Gae could easily injure her. With her body as lifeless as it was, she could have died from that Ars.

"That's my queue to leave."

The Denizens fled with a smile as he covered his body in a gold-like aura that matched the color of the flames. Anemone perceived a warm sensation flow through the entirety of her body. Her mind felt clear, and her frustration seemed to fade instantly. It was similar to the calming skill Spriggan had taught her but for a different. When she closed her eyes, she saw the sight of a female Aos-Si with eyes bluer than the sky and more remarkable than any sea appeared. They contrasted her scarlet hair, flowing in the winds painted across the horizon of a brightening sunrise. It was like someone was etching the scene of her presence in her mind.

After the calming sensation left her, the sense of tears about to pour from her eyes began. A more profound empty feeling clawed into her chest, forcing her eyes open. The sight of the cobbled road zoomed by, letting her know she was moving at an incredible speed, but she felt no motion at all. As she raised her head, buildings flew past her peripherals as unrecognizable blurs. It was as if her body was utterly senseless. When he jumped into a shadowy alley, he leaned her against a wall.

"I appreciate your compliance, your highness, and I'm sorry for being rough."

"That's rude of you to assume I had any way of complying after you did—whatever you did!

"Might want to reword that statement there. It has some dubious implications."

"You took my limp body for a ride through the town!"

"Nope, still dubious."

"You can't say what you did positively, you Dolt! I'll have you know I'm not one to fool—."

Anemone continued to yell at him as he covered her mouth. Most of it was derogatory and profane; he couldn't hear her. He placed his hand over her mouth to quiet her yelling. Slowly, her body regained its senses, and she could feel her fingers slightly fidgeting.

"Calm down, Lydia. You know I like my women emotionally unavailable and jaded by the world. Not Royal'd and Spoiled." He shrugged his shoulders. "Besides. You're a bit too young for my taste."

His eye was on her chest when he said that. She was more than offended by his statement. She knew he wasn't much older than her from the look of his face and patchy chin hairs. Also, he kept calling her Lydia, which wasn't her name. Instantly Anemone bit his hand as hard as she could. His other hand slapped his face as he covered his mouth to prevent his strident from expelling. After yanking his hand from Anemone's teeth, she quickly screamed. To which he shoved his sleeved forearm into her mouth to muzzle her.

"Hey! I said relax!"

In a muffled voice, "You tried to kill me earlier, kidnapped me, and drugged my body!"

"Well, not really. At least I was courteous—wait, kill you!?"

Anemone's irritation grew, and she vigorously chomped into his arm. It didn't take long for her jaw to begin cramping up from the width of his forearm, which she realized was surprisingly challenging for an arm. They let out a groan of pain when she bit down. His face flushed red as he pulled his arm away.

"Don't moan like that! It makes it even weirder!"

"You shoved it in my mouth, and it hurt."

"DUBIOUS IMPLICATIONS! WOMAN! Also, when did I try to kill you?

"It was less than a few hours ago! How could I possibly forget!? And what the Muspel is a woman! And who is Lydia!?"

"PFFFTT, YOU'RE L——!" His words went from a boisterous yell to a slight whisper. "Wait, You're a Sh'fae? You're not Lydia?"

"No kidding!"

He sat in front of her, saying nothing before he spoke. Although his eye was scrutinizing Anemone, they remained locked on her face. She couldn't tell what he thought since he kept a straight face the whole time.

"The last time I saw you was in the forest by your Lauma tree, and if I recall anything, you struck first, Not Lydia."

A vessel swelled in her head. "My name is Ninlil! Ninlil Anemone! Not Lydia! You murdering, kidnapping, book thief! I'd recognize that peculiar sigil anywhere. What was that Gray World?"

For a second, his face became serious. He switched back to his carefree demeanor without a beat as he stroked his chin with a tilt in his head.

"Wow, you look just like a certain herbalist. Sorry for that, but I am none of those epitaphs. Besides, there's no way that was me you saw in the woods. After I left you, I returned to that library and tried to find more information."

"I don't believe you. How else did Acaulis find you then?"

"Look, I was there while all that rumbling was going on. After I left the library, that Elf came out of nowhere, talking about a curfew and saying, I look suspicious. Next thing I know, I'm getting stabbed."

His gestures as he spoke almost seemed familiar. Anemone tried to think about how much time had passed since then. The sun had already set, and at least a few hours had passed. It meant she was unconscious for a moment, but the battle between Gallu and Spriggan might have taken longer than she expected. Acaulis chasing him down for some time wasn't too farfetched, but she didn't fully believe him. Also, she didn't know who Lydia was, and why did he say she looked just like her? In any case, Anemone was far more interested now.

"Well, Tir-noNog does have a curfew. That law is centuries old and has been there since the Gallu. Even visitors are supposed to abide by it. That aside, why do you have the same mask?"

Anemone stopped herself from continuing that thought. If Acaulis was hunting him, there was no way he was the same individual in the robe. The time didn't add up. But was he indeed a Denizen? King Cynareae, Acaulis's grandfather, was a known collector of species and often froze them for his collection. Perhaps that hobby rubbed off on his grandson. If they had remained hidden for this long, you would think someone like him would have found one and bragged about it. There was also a good chance that the Denizens remained hidden in plain sight with some Illusionary Phantasy-Ars no one knew. Anemone knew she had to get as much info out of him as possible. Thanks to his non-aggressive demeanor, she knew it would be a breeze.

"Eh, I didn't get that far into your history books." He shrugged his shoulders.

"And maybe it was another Veromanteía. Did you try stabbing *them* with the interrogation?" He poked her forehead.

"Okay, Denizen, let's say I believe you. It's been centuries since anyone has seen you and your people. You're an enigma. What's with those flames, and what's your ploy?"

"Naw, we're just really good at hiding and seek," he said dryly.

"Are you serious?"

"Mmm, yes?"

Anemone rolled her eye at his straight-faced answer. He did not express hostility so far, but she wasn't going to drop her guard. She was exhausted from the circumstances that had transgressed earlier today. But something in her made her indulge in him, and she couldn't understand why.

"Why the Muspel? Am I even complying with this conversation!?"

He smiled, replying, "Tis the power of—" and flicked his fingers. "Adnero."

A Gold Flame sparked from his hand, and its brilliance reflected in Anemone's eyes. It had no warmth, and yet it danced like any other fire. She couldn't take her eyes off how mesmerizing it was.

"And you, my friend, might be a fellow Veromanteía."

"You said that word earlier... a Vero-what now?"

"A Veromanteía, wielder of the sacred flames of Adnero, and yada yada. You might be related to a Manteía. Otherwise, you wouldn't be able to see this." He pointed at its embers.

Her eyes widened so much she could feel tears coming. She didn't know about Veromanteía or this Adnero Sibu-whatever, but she could feel connected to those black flames in her dreams, which seemed like a good hunch. Suddenly she became more interested in this Denizen and understood why Acaulis was hunting him. Had her prayers finally been answered? Was she finally going to have a quest of her own?

"Is there a black version of this odd hero? What does it do?!"

"Geez, it's Adnero. Ad-nEE-Roh. Get it right." He frowned. "I think you all call it Arcane or something. But enough of your questions. I need answers myself."

He pressed their foreheads together. Instantly Anemone's memories of Spriggan appeared at the forefront of her mind. Some of the memories were completely unfamiliar, while others were her own. Spriggan had just begun training her from when she saw things to recent times. But the foreign memories had static over them. One that stuck out most was when she was in Albion as a child. It was right after she had run away and crossed paths with Aronia for the first time. Spriggan stood next to a familiar face that carried a spade, and both struck down some crystalized creature. When he pulled his head away, the memory vanished, and out of nowhere, she saw a Fae with scarlet hair again.

"A Sh'fae with scarlet hair and azure eyes?" she mumbled.

His hand stopped and clenched her shoulders tightly. Even with her senses still numbed, she bared the pressure from his grip.

"Do you know where she is!?"

"No, I don't!" she yelled. "I saw her in... a vision."

"A vision? When did you see it? Where was she in the dream? Here? Old Tir-noNog?

"I don't know! It was after you touched me with that Od hero-whatever."

She wasn't trying to be so honest with her words, but the truth just slipped out for some reason. Trying to hide information from the Denizen felt unnatural. With her body still a bit numb, she wondered if it was the side effects of those flames. The Denizen smiled and rose to his feet without turning around. He raised his right arm as it burned with Adnero and Anemone's eyes flew to the flames like a moth. Her chest beat with fear and excitement. Like in all the books she read of heroes and Spriggan's stories. She could feel something extraordinary was about to happen. A ball of fire flew toward his burning hands. Instead of what should have been a roar of flames mixing, the fireball split into smaller embers. Hot air passed by her, and the embers scorched the wooden walls.

"I guess old Tir-noNog is my best bet. The name's L'wah, and the pleasure is all yours, Not Lydia!" He leaped back.

Anemone turned her head and saw Aronia with her wings fully spread as she flew towards him and landed a boot on his chest. His hand caught the impact of her heel, and she sent him flying out of the alley. With his initial leap and guard up, he quickly landed on his feet, switching straight into a sprint when he touched the ground.

"I leave ya alone for a few moments, and ya get yourself kidnapped!?" Aronia shouted as she darted by.

"Nia!?"

Aronia flew out of the alley with her Grimoire drawn in one hand. The Grimoire's page spread open as a magic sigil and ring expanded from its pages, and flames spiraled out like piercing arrows.

"Vulcanus-Tri: 2nd Tier: Teine Saigheadan"

Rubus came out of the alley's shadows and stood next to Anemone's still limp body.

"You're just a magnet for trouble, aren't you?" He kneeled next to her.

"No one asked you for your opinion—Wait, why are you here?"

"Acaulis started a mess we got swooped up into. Trust me. I had no other reason for being here."

A loud thud and rubble crash erupted onto the floor near Anemone. She turned to see Aronia rubbing her head.

"Did anyone get the name of the Minotaur that hit meh?"

Anemone fumbled to reach Aronia with her legs still numb. As Rubus walked past Aronia, he peeked out of the alley to see if that Denizen was still there, but he was long gone.

"Well, that was a waste of effort."

Aronia called out to Rubus, "Ye could've done more, y'know."

"I told you from the start. I wasn't trying to involve myself in more of Tirnog's issues, and I still don't."

Anemone checked Aronia's head for any injuries, but she was okay. If anything, the lack of wounds surprised her, and not a single external trauma was noticeable even though she flew through a building.

Anemone turned to Rubus. "Anyone wants to explain what's going on?"

"Before you and I had our woodland encounter with that Gallu, Clausa's envoy got attacked on the way here," Rubus explained.

Aronia continued, "I was there when Clausa arrived, along which some other cadets, including Timber. When you and Ru returned, Acaulis was duking it out with that Denizen. After they see him, everyone suddenly darts off in search of him. We joined up, and the next thing I knew, Ye got kidnapped. Again! Spriggan's going to flip."

Anemone groaned, "Seriously? If he realizes I got kidnapped again, I'll never live it down."

"Somehow, she and Acaulis have something in common," Aronia jokingly mocked.

Anemone thought to herself, "This day just keeps going."

It was the third time in a month a Gallu-Utukku attack had occurred. The unexpected delays in the trials and a stranger who could connect to her dreams also appeared. There were too many coincidences laid before her eyes. Was that stranger the masked individual from earlier, and who was that Sh'fae for whom he was searching? Was there another reason Acaulis was hunting him? She leaned back to process the overwhelming number of events stacking up, but she was tired.

Rubus began walking off. "My favor's done, Aro. I'll see you when we compete for the trials."

"Rubus," Anemone called out. "That Denizen Acaulis was chasing had the same mask as the stranger in the forest. Do you know him?

"Hmm?" Rubus stood still for a moment before he turned around. "Who are you talking about?"

"Who? Are you dense? When we were in the forest right before that, oversized Gallu would kill us."

Rubus narrowed his brows and turned to her. "You must have gotten your head knocked pretty hard by that oversized Gallu. That damn thing sent you flying with only one swing of its arm. We didn't—-" His words stopped. Soon his facial expression changed as his voice grew hushed. "What did the mask look like?"

Anemone had a clear picture of him before, but suddenly fog appeared over the replay of her memories. Her trying to remember only made the memory foggier. Instead of him standing there, he began to fade from her memories. All she saw was a cluster of scribbles where he once stood.

"I can't remember. I think it looked like...."

"Like Gray Fog."

Rubus sat in his words as he turned away without another word. Anemone saw his face flush red as he glared at her throat. "If you value your life." His voice slightly dropped. "Don't mention that to anyone else, Wingless."

Rubus never had an expression that wasn't neutral or irritated. Seeing his face this time, she didn't know what to make out of his words. A chilling feeling ran down her spine; it felt like his word held a blade to her throat. Before he said that last sentence, the red on his face would have made her think he was threatening her, but he turned pale. To see his expression flip so quickly was unnerving. Instead of questioning further, she let him walk off, thinking he'd probably kill her if she asked again. Anemone couldn't understand why he would tell her not to mention it to anyone.

Rubus being so affected by the Fog-faced individual made Anemone want to know how much he knew about him and if there was a connection to the Denizen. Now she was even more worried about tomorrow than before. Rubus was already a handful with his standoffish nature, and now it seemed as if he couldn't tolerate her even more. The effect of their dynamic would ruin their synergy as a team if she weren't careful. She was doing her best to calm herself with her breathing as the strength in her legs finally came back. Anemone stood up with Aronia leaning on her, and Aronia turned to Anemone.

"My ears were in the ringer. What were you two talking about?"

Anemone nodded, "Don't worry about it... Are you okay?"

"I'm not that dainty... but I'll be honest, we should hit the hay."

"You're right. I'm absolutely over today," Anemone groaned.

Aronia clumsily threw her arms up. "YAAASS!!!"

As Anemone helped Aronia up, they headed to Baccata's place. With the trials delayed for two days, there was little time for rest and recovery. Tomorrow, they'd probably have to help clean up the city after today's events. After all, they were still cadets and had to serve the city until further notice. But thanks to today, a glint grew in Anemone's eyes.

"The Celestials have some humor!"

THE YESTERDAY THAT BIRTHED TODAY

After viewing that scene, my body flickered. Through the Trancendant's eyes, I saw all that would befall the Land of Abhainn-Reatha; the lives lost and the decimation of the world. I saw everything that would unfold in Anemone's life, which intertwined with mine. Through Anemone's Memoria, I found who I wanted. I knew that she received the curse of immortality to find boundless knowledge. That knowledge could prevent the world's terrors and life's suffering, but she could not find it. Instead, she only found fables spread across the land, myths of tomes and celestial-like beings. But only their existence and nothing more.

When I met her, she shared her wisdom with me. I had learned so much, but now it's all so fleeting. The days spent watching her toil over her books, searching for something, sending me on an errand to find plants in obscure areas, and her over-the-top reactions brought a smile. It was just the little moments. I didn't know what words to describe how I felt, but I knew they were deep. As deep as her blood-colored hair.

"Vermillion Yuki-frigging-Hana."

Suddenly another fruit arose before me, and I could see her. Loud music bustled with a hearty tune as tons frolicked to the sound of high-note strings and flutes. Drunks yelled over which hostess had an enormous rack and was the strongest at their table. All their stained and mashed clothes matched their bustling lifestyles. Everyone was in high spirits in the scene of the tavern. Only two individuals sat at the bar with an aura that didn't match the environment, and one of them was her. They conversed in a bubble that blocked out everything that didn't involve their discussion.

Her dress made her look like a nun, and its royal blue color contrasted with her long flowing crimson hair. The oversized gold trim hat she wore covered her pale ivory face and bent her short-pointed ears to the side. Unlike the stranger next to her, he was a man. You could tell he was a man by the lack of his pointed ears because no Aos-Si lacked them. Much like her, he wore robe-like attire that was neat, clean, and untouched, exposing only his hands. His black curled hair tied back with a long sting covered a *sigil* on his back, but I knew it was the mark of a Manteía. That was the name we had before the Aos-Si called us Denizens. Both were from an era when those who used Adnero freely roamed along Aos-Si. And both of them knew me.

"The boy is going to get himself killed," he spoke. "Leave him out of our plans."

"He's almost a man... He was almost the same age you were when we met." Her eyes sharpened as she played with her hair.

"Don't remind me. I still can't believe you conned your way into my pants," he said and smiled faintly.

"Conned?" She playfully scoffed with her hand over her chest. "Why the feeling was mutual. Even if we were intoxicated and I was the aggressor."

"You're lucky Levi isn't the jealous type. But keep your mitts off his heart. He's young and inexperienced, and we shouldn't drag him into the world of mistakes we adults have made."

"Geez, Lamus, you're still a wet blanket." She threw her hands up and pouted. "He's not even my type."

"Because the only one who'd ever love you is one with no future?"

She punched him and laughed. "Alright, go back to the subject at hand."

They both laughed, and she drank two more mugs, but he paced himself through his first. His face was much more severe than hers, but you could tell she was trying to hide her feelings behind the drinks she tossed back. During their whole conversation, he never once looked her in the eye. But you could see his face become solemn after she grabbed her third drink. He placed his hand over her mug and spoke with a gentle concern as he finally looked her in the face.

"Mil? You're scared, aren't you? You only drink milk that quickly when you're overwhelmed."

She smiled and looked him in the eyes. "It's strange how you, Veromanteía, don't get drunk off milk. What do you use as liquid courage?"

"Fermented fruit. Unlike you, Snow Fae, alcohol gets us drunk, and even Levi isn't immune."

Vermillion laughed. "Does that mean even Celestials fear death?"

"I think everyone that values life does. It comes with the territory."

She twiddled her thumb and took another sip from her drink.

"Y'know, being immortal isn't all it's cracked up to be... you live life wandering the lands, trying to experience everything because you know you have all the time in the world. Muspell, you don't think about death or how your future should look. And now I suddenly have to."

Lamus moved his hand from her mug and finished his drink. Staring at his empty cup, he was at a loss for words. They had known each other for about a hundred years, crossing paths on random occasions, but she never had a look of worry on her face. Vermillion embodied a *"Blizzard in Albrecht,"* a constant force to be reckoned with, but occasionally, she was soft like snow. Vermillion was a Timeless Witch who never flinched at doing something unbelievable. They had fought beings several times their size. Scaled mountain ranges with only enough resources to last them a few days. She was wild as the wind and moved to the beat of her drum, never stopping for anyone, and yet she sat here worried about a boy only a twentieth of her age.

"How much does he know?"

"About the nigh-omnipotent elder God trying to destroy everything? Nothing. But about me? Everything."

Suddenly the world lost its color, and everything froze. Lamus could see *them* standing in the background. Even though a fog-shaped mask covered that face, he knew who was behind it. Only one other being he had crossed paths with could do such a thing, but he could not interact with the physical world. The man in the mask stood there and waved before he pointed at his wrist in some strange gesture. Lamus wondered how such a being's origins crept into their world. No one might have lived to see tomorrow if it wasn't for his father and his allies. But now, the age of Celestials was over, and heroes were few and far between. Eidolons were missing; he was the only thing left of beings who could stop his revival. As soon as the world regained its color, he turned to Vermillion.

"How long will your Never-melt last?"

"My Ice prison should have lasted a lifetime, but the boy has an amazing gift."

"That doesn't answer my question, Vermillion. How long?"

"About a hundred 100 years or so. After that, *they* became the world's problem yet again.

"Don't worry, Mil. I promise I'll find a way to stop them. After I find Levi, we'll think of something." He held her hand again. "What will you tell him?"

"Nothing... I leave L'wah with a cold shoulder." She tried to smile. "Hopefully, he'll understand. L'wah's a smart kid. He'll find a different life, a future without me."

The scene that ended made her name resonate with me. The feeling was so strong a tear rolled down my face. Unlike the other memories, I saw this one hurt me in a way that was all too familiar. The looked on that face made my chest ache so much. I knew the look of that smile more than any other smile. It was one filled with lies, pain, and suffering. Yet, it made me feel whole again. She was my master, the woman I cared for more than my safety. The Transcendent placed her hand on my face and lifted my head. Her face looked worried, and her touch was gentle. Instantly my memories came back to me. I knew who Vermillion was, how I connected to everything, and why I was here.

"My name is L'wah, and I have been searching for my "pain" of master this whole time."

She stood up and began clapping as she encircled me. The Transcendent strolled around, stretching her arms behind her back. Her steps started to flutter. The way she floated in the air as she bounced felt eerie, yet there was a triumphant smile on her face.

"Pain! Is how I'd describe her, but not for your reasons," she said, twirling away with a smile. "I felt jealousy. After that time, she sealed me up, and you locked me up for an eternity. Geez, you critters really know how to fill your closet."

"An eternity? How'd I lock you in here?"

"Oh, L'wah." She stopped bouncing. "Now that I know who I am, it doesn't matter. Cause I'm about to be free!"

I stood up, keeping my eyes locked. "You're neither Vermillion nor Anemone, are you?"

"Not entirely." She winked coyly. "Think a Lil harder."

Everything suddenly made sense to me. The reason I was here and the reason why Anemone killed me. *They* orchestrated everything. Even without directly interfering in the world, they had created the perfect opportunity to come back to life through a convoluted chain of events. A being who existed beyond the stars and brought his scourge to the world now stood before me. It was, Mehen smiling as they continued to possess Anemone's body.

"And there's nothing you can do to stop me, cycle 1047."

End of Volume 1.

About the Author

As an avid lover of anime, video games, folklore, and storytelling, Ausar has always enjoyed the fantastical worlds found in the realm of imagination and thought. Fueled by an appreciation for mythology and science, he hopes to create worlds that represent the voices of those who have yet to tell their stories. His philanthropic work with young men of color and personal experience as a BIPOC has become the backbone for telling stories of Lore and Yore.

Social media links

Instagram @ Ausar_Imani

vero.ausar.imani@gmail.com

Facebook @ The False Fae [1]

Book Preview: Ausar_Imani - Wattpad [2]

Page |

---

1. https://www.facebook.com/profile.php?id=100086982370893

2. https://www.wattpad.com/user/OsirusFulton